The Seventh Ward

The Haunted Series

Book 2

Patrick Logan

Books by Patrick Logan

The Haunted Series

Book 1: Shallow Graves

Book 2: The Seventh Ward

Book 3: Seaforth Prison

Book 4: Scarsdale Crematorium

Insatiable Series

Book 1: Skin

Book 2: Crackers

Book 3: Flesh

Book 4: Parasite

Book 5: Stitches (Spring 2017)

Family Values Trilogy

Witch (Prequel)

Mother

Father

Daughter (Spring 2017)

Short Stories

System Update

Prologue

"HEY, DANNY, YOU ALMOST done over there?"

Danny pulled the headphones out of his ears, then switched off the floor cleaner.

"What? You say something?"

He eyed his friend from across the hall. Lawrence was tall, thin, and had a perpetually goofy expression on his narrow face. Big ears, big eyes, big mouth pretty much summed him up.

"I asked if you were done," Lawrence replied. He balled up the paper towel that he had been using to clean the silver gurney and tossed it into the waste bin.

"Almost..." Danny waved a hand, indicating the thin strip of dirty floor on the other side of the hallway. "Just have to do that strip and then I'm done—we can pack it up then."

A quick glance at the Timex on his wrist revealed that it was nearly three in the morning. "Yeah, let's stop at three."

Lawrence smiled at him, revealing a set of large, almost buck teeth.

"Then can we go check out that ward?"

Danny made a face.

"What ward?"

Lawrence rolled his eyes and tore off another sheet of paper towel.

"Don't be coy—you know what ward."

Danny's eyes narrowed and he grimaced.

"No," he said simply, jamming his headphones back into his ears before his friend could complain. He knew that Lawrence was talking, but with his music blaring, he couldn't make out the words, which was fine by him. After switching the floor cleaner back on, and feeling the vibrations that traveled up his arms, he couldn't hear Lawrence at all.

As Danny maneuvered the device toward the dirty strip in the hallway, which was also the final hallway in the Eighth Ward of Pinedale Hospital that required cleaning, he let his mind wander.

Why are we cleaning this place again?

After all, the hospital had been abandoned for years…a decade or more. Not a native of Corgin, two weeks ago Danny had never even heard of the place. After a little research, however, he thought that the blond man in the suit was pulling his leg.

Clean an abandoned hospital? What for?

At the time, the man's response had been convincing enough: they were thinking of turning it into some sort of museum, an archive of old-fashioned equipment from the mid to late nineties. But glancing around now, Danny couldn't see anything that remotely resembled museum-worthy pieces. In fact, most of the medical equipment had been removed, presumably by the company that had packed up the hospital in the first place, or by looters. What was left wasn't *'antique,'* but just shit. Even his inexperienced mind knew that.

After all, most of his experience had come in the form of cleaning it up.

The fact that Danny Dekeyser had been approached by the man at all had been a surprise. Cleaning an entire hospital, a total of eight wards, was a massive job, and all he had was himself and Lawrence to do the work. Truthfully, one of the much larger, commercial companies would have been a better fit, and Danny had nearly said as much. But with his medical bills piling up and the numbers that the stranger in the suit was throwing around, how could he refuse? Especially with a wife and daughter to support.

The floor cleaner suddenly chuffed, and Danny looked around the side to make sure it hadn't snagged on anything. There was something pink, like a wad of gum, stuck halfway out of the hard red bristles. He moved the brush-wheel back and forth aggressively over the spot a few times, but whatever it was, it refused to unglue from the floor.

"Fuck," he grumbled, slipping the scraper from the loop on his belt. He shut off the buffer and pulled it off the pink wad. As he squatted to start scraping, he heard Lawrence mumbling, and he reluctantly pulled one of the buds out of his ears.

"What?" he said without turning.

"Fuck, man, you gotta turn that shit down. Not good for your ears."

Danny said nothing.

"Jesus, you're in a mood today, aren't you?"

Danny stared at the three-inch-long piece of gum or whatever the hell it was for a second, his eyes defocusing.

He slid the scraper under the one side, which was thicker than the other, and gave it a little push.

"Danny?"

Danny shook his head and turned to his friend.

"Sorry, man. Just tired, is all. I want to go home, have a beer, put my dogs up."

He had been feeling off lately, and was trying his best not to think about the prospect of the cancer returning. It had been in remission for nearly two years, but his doctor had said he would never quite be out of the woods. And ever since he had accepted the job at Pinedale Hospital, he had been feeling run-down, which was exactly how he had felt before his initial diagnosis.

"Yeah, man, I hear ya," Lawrence responded. His goofy face went serious for a second, and Danny knew what the man was thinking, because he was thinking it too.

He shrugged.

"It's nothing, maybe a cold—the flu. Fuck, I'll be fine." Then he smiled. A weak smile, but a smile nonetheless.

The goofy grin on Lawrence's lips returned and he made his thick eyebrows dance.

"I thought I heard something."

Danny pulled the other headphone out.

"Now?"

"No, not now. Before, when I was yelling your name for like five minutes."

Danny shook his head, thinking back to the blond man in the suit handing over the set of keys—archaic things that looked as ancient as some of the leftover equipment—and the keycards. The keys got you into the building, but from there, in order to get around, you needed to use the keycards.

"There's no one else here."

"Heard a door close." His grin grew. "Below us."

Now it was Danny's turn to roll his eyes. What had happened in Pinedale about five years before it shut down had become something of an urban legend, and although Danny hadn't even heard of the place before, a quick Internet search had revealed plenty.

Mostly—maybe all—bullshit, something about a psychiatric inmate butchering another patient and a doctor, trying to prove some insane theory of his.

Danny believed none of it. Lawrence, on the other hand, was obsessed.

Let's go find the Seventh Ward, he would start each night with, and Danny would tell him no.

The man in the suit's instructions were explicitly clear: they were supposed to start on the top floor, on the Eighth Ward. The cancer ward, ironically. And then they were to make their way down. Leave it to Lawrence to point out that the ward numbers jumped from six to eight.

Only once had Danny, during a rare moment of weakness, allowed Lawrence to go exploring. Stranger still was the fact that he had gone with his friend.

In the basement, they had found a single door, the only one in the entire hospital, as far as he could tell, that was unlabeled. And neither of the keycards that the man had given them would open it.

This is the Seventh Ward, Lawrence had said giddily, to which Danny had promptly replied that it was probably just storage.

Danny stifled a cough and swallowed the phlegm that filled his mouth.

"There's no one here," he said, turning back to the floor. His gloved hand brushed against the pink thing. It was surprisingly soft, pliable even.

What the fuck?

Even the layers of dust in the abandoned hospital had their own layers of dust; the doors had been closed for years.

But this...this pink thing appeared fresh...organic even. It looked strangely like a finger, a smooth, pink finger with no nail on the end.

Danny made a disgusted face.

Maybe...maybe Lawrence was —

But the door to the cancer ward was suddenly thrown wide, cutting off all rational thought. Danny's head shot up so quickly that he lost his balance and fell backward, smacking his tailbone on the floor.

"Wha—wha—?" he stammered, trying to catch his bearings.

Lawrence cried out when a lumbering shadow emerged from the open door.

"Danny?"

Swallowing hard, Danny managed to regain a modicum of control and pushed himself to his feet.

"Who is it?" he demanded, trying to sound authoritative. "You're not supposed to be here."

His words came out meek despite his efforts.

They only had two work lights, both running on a set of lithium-ion batteries: one was splashed against the hallway wall so that Danny could see where he was cleaning, while Lawrence was using the other to clean the gurneys. Neither were pointed at the door at the end of the hall, leaving that area basking in darkness.

As it was, Danny could only make out a shadow in the doorway.

But then the figure stepped into the light, and Danny felt his heart rate double.

He was huge, bigger than any man that Danny had ever seen—at least six feet six, maybe even taller. But that wasn't the most shocking thing about him.

The man was *fragmented* somehow…all hard angles, none of his features matching up perfectly. Thick, lace-like stitches crisscrossed his massive barrel chest, which had—*Jesus Christ*—a single, purple and deformed breast sutured to the center. The man's right arm was proportionate, but the left was considerably smaller, and while the former was a pale gray, the latter was a dark, pigmented brown.

And that said nothing of the mess between his legs.

"Wha—what—you—you can't be in here," Danny stammered. His grip instinctively tightened on the metal scraper.

The man laughed and bounded awkwardly toward him, failing to notice Lawrence, who had since slunk behind his trolley full of cleaning supplies.

Danny froze in place as the man neared.

He was even more hideous up close, his face a mishmash of different features, none of which seemed to fit: a dark, black nose, bent slightly to the right; the skin surrounding his left eye pink, as if sunburned. His mouth was a jagged slit that continued nearly to his ear on the left side, the stitches having since separated.

It was like Frankenstein's monster, only more hideous.

And it was real.

"What the fuck—you can't—"

"The name is George," the man said. When he spoke, the stitches in his face separated even more, revealing a row of rotting yellow molars.

Danny wanted to run—he wanted to turn and get the fuck out of there as fast as humanly possible. But he couldn't.

It was as if his feet were encased in ice.

The man continued his approach, his gait awkward, lumbering, as if one leg was a few inches shorter than the other. And the worst part was that Danny thought that maybe this was the case, but he was too scared to look away from the man's dark, black eyes to check.

As George traversed the short distance between them, Danny started to pick up a general funk, a rotting smell that soon became so pungent that it made his eyes water.

When he was only two feet away, George suddenly stopped, his eyes narrowing. At first Danny thought that he was staring at him, but then he lowered his gaze and chuckled.

"There it is," he said. The monster bent at the waist, revealing more of the thick, shoelace-like stitches that crisscrossed his back.

George groaned and grabbed the pink thing that Danny had been trying to remove from the floor. With a yank, he pulled it off the ground. Then he brought it up to eye level and studied it for a moment before chuckling again.

"That's where that went."

Then he showed Danny his left hand...and the missing thumb. Like a magician pulling a parlor trick, he raised the pink appendage up and moved it back and forth from where it had been amputated.

Danny's stomach lurched and he could feel his whole body tense. Sweat broke out on his brow.

The man's face suddenly went serious.

"You hear that?"

Danny swallowed hard and gaped at the human freak show before him. It couldn't be real, of course. It had to be the cancer coming back. The first time he had been diagnosed, and shortly after starting chemo, he remembered wild, vivid dreams. Even during the day, he would occasionally have minor hallucinations.

Nothing as horrific as this, of course, but it just couldn't possibly be real.

"I said, did you hear that?" George asked again, his voice deepening, becoming more aggressive. No matter how intimidating the man was, Danny still couldn't bring himself to answer.

George leaned in closer now to within three inches of Danny, and it was all he could do not to vomit.

The man's breath reeked of rotting fish, and that said nothing of the horrific details of his face: the stitches, the patchwork skin that had so clearly been scavenged from other people. And judging by the smell, it had been none too fresh when it had been harvested.

"I think it was the Goat," George hissed. "I heard he was coming."

A shout suddenly erupted from somewhere behind George.

"I don't know who the fuck—" But before Lawrence could finish his sentence, something flashed in Danny's periphery.

The broom handle came down in a swooping arc. It thwacked against George's segmented back, and the man straightened, pulling away from Danny, taking his awful, rotting breath with him.

He grunted and started to turn. The way he moved was awful, the patchwork skin all possessed with different plasticity, bending and folding and creasing independently.

"You shouldn't have done that," he whispered. Lawrence reared back to swing the broom again, when Danny finally snapped out of his stupor.

"No! Don't!" he shouted, but he was too late.

George grabbed the broom from Lawrence with the hand that still had a thumb, and in one sharp tug, he pulled it from his grasp.

"You shouldn't have done that," George repeated.

Danny wanted to do something, *would* have done something to help his friend, but he was too slow. With his other hand, George reached out and grasped Lawrence by the throat. Even without a thumb, the man's grip was so strong that Lawrence couldn't peel it away even with both hands.

Gasping, Danny stood helplessly and watched his friend begin to thrash as he was lifted clean off the floor.

"He's coming...he's coming...he's coming..." George began to repeat over and over again.

It was then that Danny realized that he was still gripping the paint scraper in his hand. He raised it slowly, almost robotically, with the intention of driving it into George's neck, when Lawrence's eyes suddenly started to cloud over, to turn completely black.

Danny Dekeyser dropped the paint scraper and ran.

***

With only his small penlight to lead him, Danny couldn't find his way to the front door of Pinedale Hospital. Instead, he found himself moving deeper into the bowels of the hospital, trying to get far enough away that he could no longer hear Lawrence's screams.

Eventually, he found himself at a door—the door that he and Lawrence had tried to open a week ago, but had failed. In his desperation, however, this slipped his mind. His outstretched hands found the door handle and he gripped it furiously, rattling it up and down, all the while banging his shoulder against it. It wouldn't open. And then his penlight blinked out.

"Fuck," he whispered into the pitch blackness.

His hand went to his hip next, grabbing the keycard that was attached via a retractable cord. He yanked it hard, and then blindly waved the card in the area that he assumed the reader was. At first nothing happened, and his nearly overwhelming panic started to become a crescendo. In his mind, he could hear George's heavy, thumping footsteps, one hard, one light.

"C'mon, c'mon," he muttered, now waving the card aimlessly in the dark.

Just when he was going to release the retractable cord and move deeper into the hospital to search for an area that was better lit by the moonlight, he heard a muted beep and a small green LED light cut through the darkness.

Yes!

Danny yanked on the door and pulled it wide, quickly stepping inside. He closed it behind him, then raised his head to where he thought the pane of glass was. Even though he couldn't see anything in the darkness, knowing that he was staring out of the window, offered him some comfort.

For a long while, the only noise that Danny heard was the sound of his own breathing. As his heart rate began to normalize, he was suddenly overcome with the urge to cough. He brought a hand to his mouth and pressed his lips together as hard as he could in an attempt to stifle it.

Given the tightness in his chest and lungs, Danny did a fairly good job of holding back; only spit sprayed from his lips.

The problem was, even during his stifled spurts, he continued to hear the same rhythmic breathing.

Only now he was sure it wasn't his.

Danny, eyes wide, desperately seeking something, anything, in the utter blackness, whipped around, his back pressing up against the door.

Then he smelled it again: the unmistakable odor of rot.

"Welcome to the Seventh Ward, Danny. I've been waiting for you."

PART I - Another Letter, Another Job

Chapter 1

ROBERT WATTS LEANED BACK from his computer and rubbed his eyes. Despite spending more than a decade looking at numbers on a computer screen, he just didn't have the stamina for it anymore.

Something had happened to him after he'd left Audex; he had slowly lost his patience with cellphones and other electronic devices. In fact, the Harlop Estate didn't even have a TV, much to Cal's chagrin.

Shelly, on the other hand, didn't seem to care either way.

The only thing that Robert couldn't do without was Wi-Fi, which was why fitting the place with a solid Internet connection was one of the first things he had done since moving in.

Robert blinked long and slow, forcing his eyes to water a bit, trying to alleviate the visual fatigue. When his focus returned, he found himself staring at the simple photograph of Amy in the frame on his desk. Although he couldn't remember getting it taken—maybe Wendy had had done it—it must have been an extra passport photograph. Amy wasn't smiling in it, as any form of expression in these photos was not permitted, but nothing could take the smile and joy that filled her eyes.

A pang of sadness hit him somewhere deep in the pit of his stomach, but before it could worm itself into full blown depression, he gritted his teeth and shook the feeling away. Eager to distract himself now, Robert leaned forward in his chair and went back to what he found himself doing most days now: browsing the Internet for information on the Marrow.

Despite being flooded with more useless information than he thought possible, information on the Marrow was exceedingly sparse. He had amassed more information than Cal and Shelly had come up with, but not much else. One thing that had remained consistent, however, was Shelly's initial claim that no one had actually been there and returned to speak about it, which would explain the paucity of information.

Except for him, of course, which was something that Robert continued to keep to himself, and would do so until he was completely satisfied that revealing this wouldn't put Cal or Shelly in any danger.

About a week ago, Robert had come across something interesting, something surprisingly credible. A couple of hidden back links on a site about the afterlife had led him to an obscure fishing bulletin board. One of the first things that Robert had figured out while searching the Internet was that it wasn't so much *what* you looked for but *where*. He had found information about the Marrow hiding out in an online walkthrough guide for Doom the videogame and even in the comments on a random wedding photo album. So while others might have logged out of the fishing bulletin board, he didn't.

And he was glad that he had stayed, because it was here that he had first discovered a mysterious cyber identity that went by the handle 'LBlack'. As he read through the man's posts, it became clear that he knew what he was talking about.

The devil was in the details, so they said, and nothing could have been more true in this instance. The way LBlack described the foamy Marrow sea, the way it broke over the soft, pillowy sand, the sound of the rolling waves…it was exactly the way

Robert remembered it. While others reported something similar, the detail that LBlack went into was such that Robert was convinced that the man had been there.

And it was also that he had mentioned the thunder in the sky, the impending storm. Robert could still remember how that felt, how, peering upward, the serenity that had so engulfed his very quiddity had suddenly fallen away. How the lightning that split the clouds seemed to leave a fissure behind, and in that fissure, he could hear the most horrible...

A scream from somewhere below caused him to bolt upright in his chair.

"Cal? Shelly?" he hollered.

All he could hear was Shelly's rock music playing, and for a moment he thought that maybe he had just imagined the cry, that it was part of his reverie of the Marrow.

"Cal?" he asked, raising his voice a few octaves. When the only response was the sound of crashing cymbals and bass riffs, Robert rose from his chair and made his way to the office entrance. He peered out, hoping to see Cal and Shelly laughing over a few drinks.

But no one was standing outside the room, nor was there anybody in the hallway.

Robert couldn't remember whose idea it had been to all move into the Harlop Estate, but at the time it had made sense. After all, Robert had no place to live, Cal was a roaming nomad, and Shelly, who was ironically from Montreal, of all places, was in the process of moving and had her house already up on the market. They had used the proceeds from the sale of her place to pay off what remained of Robert's bills — *Wendy's* bills — and then they had all moved in.

A temporary solution, they had agreed, but over the past few months they had become one strange, blended family.

Robert had set up his office on the second floor, hoping to do some freelance accounting work on the side until he got something more permanent in Hainsey County. After all, even with no mortgage or debt, they still needed money to live. For starters, they had to keep the lights on and the Internet working, lest they forget food and entertainment. And whoever had been paying the electric company before they had arrived—he had a sneaking suspicion that it was a man with short blond hair and a black suit—had stopped ever since the deed was transferred over.

Problem was, there wasn't much accounting work out there, and over the past few months, Robert found himself spending more time researching the Marrow more than posting on freelance accounting sites. As for Cal and Shelly…well, they spent most of their time talking about conspiracy theories and drinking. Which was fine by him…for now. But soon they would need a steady form of income. If they were going to make this work at the Harlop Estate, they had to become cashflow positive—and soon.

Another scream bounced off the high ceilings and Robert flicked back into the moment, his heart racing. He leaned over the railing and peered down, trying to locate his housemates. He was suddenly reminded of the scream that little Patricia had made when she had been shoved from the roof.

"Cal! What the—?"

But then he saw Shelly step out from the sitting room to the base of the massive staircase.

"Shelly, what's wrong?"

But Shelly didn't turn to look up at him. Instead, she just continued to back up slowly, her finger outstretched, her other hand cupping her mouth. Her face was deathly pale, her eyes wide.

"Shelly!" he shouted. He turned, intent on running down the stairs and going to her, when she pulled her hand away from her mouth and held it up to him, staying his forward advance.

Robert swallowed hard.

"What—what is it?" he asked, his voice barely a whisper now. Somewhere in the back of his mind, he realized that the music had stopped.

Shelly took another few steps backward, still pointing at something that Robert couldn't see.

"It's—it's—" she stammered.

Robert heard a new sound: the rusty, creaking sound of worn metal.

"—it's Ruth, she's back!" Shelly finished in a gasp.

Robert felt his legs go numb. Even if he'd wanted to, if Shelly had lowered her hand and waved him down to her, he wouldn't have been able to.

He was frozen with fear.

And when the rusted wheel of Ruth Harlop's wheelchair came into view with her gnarled, leathery hand gripping the worn rubber, a scream rose in his throat.

Chapter 2

"DOCTOR, YOUR NEWEST PATIENT has arrived," the portly nurse informed him in a soft voice.

Dr. George Mansfield pulled the glasses off his nose and let them fall to his neck where they rested from the cord. He gave the nurse a quick onceover, his dark eyes darting first to her nametag, which read *Justine Sinclair*, before observing the rest of her. She was a doughy woman, pasty and thick throughout, especially her lower half. The doctor didn't recognize her, which meant she was one of the new nurses that had been sent to him on rotation following his written complaints of chronic understaffing.

Just another virgin cutting her teeth in the Pinedale Psych Ward, or as it was more commonly referred to, the Seventh Ward. He hoped that, unlike the others, she would last longer than a week.

"Doctor?" Justine asked slowly, averting her eyes as embarrassment from his overt observation took hold.

She was a wholly unattractive woman—upturned nose, thin lips, hair that was cut to shoulder length and dry to the point of being frizzy.

"Nurse, if me staring at you is going to make you embarrassed, you should probably look for another job."

"Oh, I'm...I'm sorry, Doctor, I just—"

"Seriously."

Justine's eyes darted up again. Although her cheeks were still red, her eyes became clear, focused.

"Yes, sir."

Dr. Mansfield took the file from her outstretched hand and flipped it open.

"This isn't medieval times, Justine. Don't call me 'sir.' Call me 'Doctor.'"

This time, the nurse didn't respond, and Dr. Mansfield put his glasses back on and quickly scanned the file.

Twenty-four-year-old medical student experienced a mental break-down. Potential past psych issues, suspected bipolar. Spent two weeks in the hospital following most recent episode, diagnosed with fatigue and general malaise. During recovery, started to express two separate personalities: one, the doting medical student, quiet, shy, obedient to a fault. Personality two: angry, irate, irrational. Vengeful. Arrogant.

Dr. Mansfield reread the first page of the report, his interest piqued.

A medical student with a split personality? That's a new one.

He flipped over to the next page, aware, but not caring, that Justine was still staring at him.

A photograph was affixed to the top of this page, a headshot of a young man with shaggy brown hair and small eyes beset in dark circles. His nose was slightly crooked, his ears just a little too large. But on the whole, he was average-looking.

Dr. Mansfield supposed with another few hours of sleep a night, and maybe a career change, he might be boosted to above average.

Beneath the photograph was a list of specific incidents—a step-by-step account of the events that had led the internist to send the patient to the Seventh Ward. Dr. Mansfield glossed over these details; in his many years of working with psych patients, he often found that not only were these reports not help-ful, but they often proved detrimental to his analysis. They ei-ther biased him, or they were just simply inaccurate to the point of being distracting. The most blatant case in recent memory was of a forty-year-old broker who'd just woken up one night screaming, one of those obnoxious, high-pitched screams, every few minutes for no discernible reason. The emergency department had referred the man to the Seventh Ward after a routine exam revealed nothing physically wrong with him. Their official diagnosis had been 'classic mental breakdown, likely owing to stress.'

You know, high pressure job and all that.

But Dr. Mansfield thought differently. And, sure enough, a more thorough examination revealed an inch-long millipede burrowed deep in the man's ear canal. Filling the ear with a little alcohol, and applying a little gentle coaxing with a pair of tweezers, and the offending insect had fallen right out.

The screaming had stopped immediately, and the man had returned to normal—his incredible gratitude notwithstanding.

Dr. Mansfield snapped the folder closed and handed it back to Justine.

"You don't want to read any more?" she asked.

He sighed, removed his glasses again, and stared at her. As the seconds ticked by, the nurse became increasingly uncomfortable, shifting her considerable weight from one foot to another.

Eventually, Dr. Mansfield broke the silence.

"Justine—you need to remain firm, confident. Did the other nurses give you a tour already?"

The woman nodded, the thick skin beneath her chin waddling.

"And did they tell you how dangerous some of our patients can be?"

Again she nodded, but with less certainty this time.

Dr. Mansfield sighed again.

"I'm going to be honest with you, Justine, because skirting the truth is not only dishonest, but in this place—" He waved his arms, indicating the pale gray walls of the Seventh Ward. "—in this place, you let your guard down for one second, just one, and not only can you be severely injured or even killed, but your brain can become infected."

Justine stared at him, her eyes widening. He couldn't tell if it was fear or incredulity in those dark pits, but for her sake, Dr. Mansfield hoped the former.

"Look, I've spent seventeen years dealing with psych patients of all different types, ranging from the demure and docile to the hyper-violent. Most outsiders think that these patients are stupid, that their mental proclivities make them idiotic. But that couldn't be further from the truth. These people…what's the best way of putting this? These psychiatric patients are in a way *unburdened* by the constraints of society. Because of this, they lock on to an idea, any idea, and it *becomes* them. They are *obsessed* in the truest sense of the word—completely intractable." He paused, still staring into Justine's eyes. "Do you understand?"

Justine started to nod again, but Dr. Mansfield stopped her by holding up his hand.

"Nodding won't cut it this time," he informed her. "You need to say it."

Justine swallowed hard.

"Yes, I understand, Doctor."

"Good. Because these ideas that the patients of the Seventh Ward cherish are very powerful. If you let your guard down even for a moment, you too can become infected. I've seen it happen before, Justine. You need to take this seriously."

Dr. Mansfield saw the woman's thin lips move, making the word 'infected.'

There is no way that she makes it through the week.

Still, they were short-staffed, and he had no choice but to use her as much as he could while she was still around.

"Do you understand?" he repeated.

"Yes," Justine replied, more strongly this time. "I understand, Dr. Mansfield."

"Good, now please, take me to my newest patient."

Justine nodded, and then turned awkwardly, leading the way down the hall to the room with the large *ADMITTING* sign above. She pushed through the swinging doors, flashing the ID card that hung around her neck to the tall black security guard who stood off to one side, his arms crossed over his chest. The man nodded and waved them through.

"Here he is," Justine informed him, gesturing with a chubby hand to the man strapped to the gurney.

Dr. Mansfield slowly moved up next to the man, making a mental note that the four straps, one on each limb, were tightly affixed.

Good. At least the nurse got that part right.

A med student with a split personality didn't immediately ring alarm bells in his head, but he had learned that these patients could be wildly unpredictable.

Better safe than sorry.

Dr. Mansfield stared at the man's face, which was so eerily similar to the photograph in the folder that it looked as if it could have been taken just moments ago.

"Hi there," he said softly.

The man opened his eyes and a thin smile crossed his pale face.

"Hello—" Dr. Mansfield reached over and grabbed the folder from Nurse Justine and read the cover quickly. "—hello Andrew Shaw. Welcome to the Seventh Ward."

Chapter 3

"YOU ARE A FUCKING asshole, you know that?"

Cal tried to stop laughing, but he couldn't. He pressed his lips together, which stifled the sound for a few seconds, but then he exploded in a spray of spit and tears. His hands went to his belly and he keeled over.

Robert, on the other hand, was far from amused.

"What's wrong with you?" He walked over to the wheelchair and picked up the rubber hand and threw it at Cal. It hit him in the shoulder, but instead of angering him, this only served to make him laugh even harder.

Shelly, who was standing by the entrance to the sitting room, suddenly started giggling too, and Robert whipped around to face her. The reason why she had been able to pull this ruse off was in part because she had covered her face in some sort of white paint, or powder, or something.

"And you? You think this is funny too?"

Shelly averted her eyes and managed to control herself—she was still smiling, but at least she wasn't laughing anymore.

"It's Halloween, Rob, and it was just a joke. Lighten up a bit."

The fact that it was Halloween came as a surprise to Robert. Out here in Hainsey County, at the Harlop Estate, time moved more slowly. It wasn't like it had been in the basement, but instead of seconds and minutes, the days all seemed to meld together, trickling like molasses through a bendy straw.

October 31st? We've been living here for nearly three months?

It hadn't felt half that long.

Robert scowled and shook his head.

It didn't matter if it was Halloween, or Christmas, or Yom Kippur.

"You want me to lighten up?" He gestured to Shelly and then Cal, who was still laughing. "Maybe you two should get a little more serious."

"Rob—" Shelly began, but Robert cut her off.

"No, don't start that 'Rob' stuff. You want to know the truth? Well, I'll tell you the truth. I've been running some numbers— yeah, I can still do accounting—and we can maybe last 'till the end of the year with no more income. That's it. Two full months. Then what? Have you thought of that? Maybe, instead of practical jokes, you two could think of something to do to make some money, huh?"

Shelly pressed her red lips together in defiance. He knew that he only had a moment before she came back with a biting retort, which would lead to a fight that wouldn't end well. Probably worse for him. But he was still fuming.

Really? A dead woman? Pretending that the fucking dead woman that I thought I had killed was still hanging around? The one that we hadn't sent her ghost to the Marrow? That's funny? What about Amy? Going to pretend she's still hanging around too?

Robert felt his lower lids start to tingle and knew that tears would soon follow. He ground his teeth, trying to force them away.

"Hey, Robbo, I'm sorry, okay?" Cal said, finally stopping laughing. "We didn't mean anything by it."

Robert sniffed and wiped at his nose. When he spoke again, some of the anger had fled him.

"Yeah, well, it wasn't fucking funny."

Cal held up his hands defensively.

"Fine. Sorry. Thought it would lighten the mood a bit. You've been...serious—so serious lately." Cal jabbed at his chest with a chubby index finger. "Not good for the old ticker."

Robert ignored the comment and turned to Shelly, expecting her to apologize as well. When none was forthcoming, he knew he should have known better. Shelly was standing with her hands on her hips now, her lips still pushed together as if to say, 'how dare you speak to me this way.'

He shook his head and closed his eyes. If there was one saving grace to her intractable stubbornness, it was that he was no longer on the verge of bursting into tears.

Cal quickly moved between them.

"You want a drink, Robbo?"

Robert gave his friend a onceover.

His wide-set eyes were soft, caring. Clearly, the gag wasn't meant as something cruel, just a practical joke gone wrong.

Maybe if you weren't so wrapped up in this stuff about the Marrow...

Robert shook the thought away.

No, joking about the dead is never right — Halloween or not.

Cal went to put his arm around him, but Robert shrugged him off.

"No, I don't want one right now... I think — I think I'm going to go for a walk."

Cal turned his attention to the window.

"It's pitch black out," he stated matter-of-factly.

Robert followed his gaze. Living at the Harlop Estate wasn't like living in the city; when it got dark in Hainsey, it got *very* dark. And ever since what had happened with the Harlops, he had become leery of the dark, thinking that he could hear things in it, a rat scurrying, nails on wood. But tonight, however, he felt the need to get outside, to get a little exercise. He had to clear his head, and not just because of the distasteful gag.

"Doesn't matter."

Robert made his way toward the massive wooden doors and grabbed his jacket off the clothes rack by the entrance. He pulled the scarf out of the sleeve and wrapped it around his neck before putting on his coat.

"I'm going out anyway. Be back in an hour or so."

He unlatched the door and then pulled it wide.

"Hey, Robbo?"

Robert turned, and was surprised to see Cal smiling again.

"It was a pretty good one, though, wasn't it?"

"Fuck off," Robert replied, before slamming the wooden door to the Harlop Estate behind him.

***

It was Halloween, but Robert didn't expect to see any trick-or-treaters on this night. Not with the house being as isolated as it was. He turned back to stare at the Harlop Estate, and suddenly felt sad...sad and lonely. Part of him wished that there *were* trick-or-treaters, some young laughs and cries to liven the place up.

To remind him of Amy, however painful that might be.

And, besides, the Harlop Estate would make one hell of a haunted house.

It wasn't quite as frightening as it had been when he and Amy had first arrived, but it was impressive, especially at night. The three of them had scrubbed the Xs off the eyes of the cherub out front, and they had filled the basin with fresh water. He had also continued to do some landscaping, trimming hedges, pulling weeds from the cracked stones, but this he had done alone. To their credit, both Cal and Shelly had offered to help, but he had refused. It was his alone time, a distraction from thinking about their finances or the Marrow, to just remember how he and Amy used to do it, even if back then she hadn't really been *there*. But the rest of the estate? Doing anything about the cracked exterior far exceeded their paygrades and experience levels, and it was too big to paint.

So, yeah, it would have freaked the crap out of any kids that made it up to the door. And the wheelchair and fake hand? That would have been the icing on the cake.

Robert suddenly felt bad for the way he had exploded at Cal and Shelly, but lately he could feel his stress levels rising. Even though the Harlop family was gone, he still didn't feel perfectly normal in the house.

What had Cal said? *Are you feeling weird? Getting angry more quickly than usual?*

Something like that...the truth was, he *did* find himself flying off the handle more than usual. And with only the two of them around, they often fell victim to his frustrations.

It was just that there were so many questions bouncing around in his brain, questions that he just couldn't rouse up nearly enough satisfactory answers for.

Robert tucked his hands deep into the pockets of his jacket as a gust of wind struck him. It was unseasonably cold out, he realized, and he hoped that the snow would hold off for as long as possible. What he had said about their finances had been true, but if the snow came early, or it was a particularly cold fall, heating the massive estate would only serve to blow through their paltry resources.

Before even realizing it, he had made his way down to the front gate. The gate had proven to be another point of frustration for him, as no matter how much olive oil or grease or WD-40 they applied to the hinges, the damn thing wouldn't open more than five feet. Robert reached over and pressed the button

on the inside of the gate, preparing himself for the awful grind-
ing sound that was coming.

The screech cut through the night air, a strange surrogate for
children's joyful, frightened Halloween cries, and Robert
pulled his hands out of his pockets and covered his ears. After
a full minute of the horrible noise, the gate finally came to a stop
and he slipped through the opening. He debated closing it, but
that would mean hearing the horrible noise three more times,
something he didn't want to do.

He left it open.

Head down, Robert started walking down the empty street,
lost in thought. It was, as Cal had said, near-pitch black out, his
path only illuminated by the pale moonlight.

And the glowing cherry of a lit cigarette twenty yards away.

What the—?

A man stepped out of the shadows and Robert froze.

"You!"

Chapter 4

FOURTEEN YEARS AGO

NURSE JUSTINE MADE IT through the first week just fine, if a bit tentative. In fact, she was well into her second month as a full-time Seventh Ward nurse. In this case, and only this case, Dr. Mansfield didn't mind being wrong. And the truth was, for all of his reservations from their initial encounter, the woman was actually useful, which was saying something considering how jaded some of the other, more experienced nurses had become. But that wasn't the only good news that brightened his mood; in fact, it paled in comparison to the news surrounding his newest patient.

Although his initial interviews had revealed that there *was* something to Andrew Shaw, something hidden just below the surface, he wasn't certain that it was a violent second personality. Time and further interviews would tell, and there was certainly enough evidence to commit Andrew, but this was no bug-in-the-ear scenario. And, like Justine, the man was actually smart and *helpful*. Obedient, docile, and more knowledgeable of psychiatric disorders and symptoms than any third-year medical student he had ever met before.

Low staffed as the Seventh Ward was, it wasn't long before Dr. Mansfield invited Andrew to come along with him for his daily rounds. Together they would interview other patients, and at first Andrew did nothing but observe. Which was fine by Dr. Mansfield; in fact, it was something that he would have insisted should Andrew have attempted to interact with the patients in this capacity. He made damn sure to make it clear that Andrew was also admitted, that he was a patient and not a doctor. It was a non-traditional approach, to be sure, and likely flew in the face of a half dozen protocols, but Dr. Mansfield was the psychiatrist-in-chief and he needed all the help he could get. And besides, he thought that this treatment would actually help the man's condition, however clandestine.

After a particularly difficult case—a young woman with at least sixteen documented personalities—Dr. Mansfield found himself in the staff lounge for a much-needed cup of coffee. He was nearing the end of a fourteen-hour shift, and he was particularly exhausted. Usually after seeing patients with Andrew tagging along, he made sure to send him back to his room— reinforcing the notion that he was indeed a patient. But this time, it slipped his mind, and now he found himself pouring two cups of coffee—one for him, and one for Andrew Shaw.

"So? What do you think, Andrew?"

The man looked so surprised to be called upon that at first he only gaped.

Dr. Mansfield's query served two purposes: one, to see if he could find any more cracks in the veneer that he had first identified when Andrew had arrived; and, two, he was genuinely interested in what the man had to say.

He really had shown some insight over the past month or so.

"Andrew? What do you think of Giselle Stall? Any opinions on her split personality disorder?"

Again, Andrew didn't answer. Instead, he chewed the inside of his lip for so long that Dr. Mansfield had started to think that maybe it would be better to send him back to his room after all. But then he spoke, and Dr. Mansfield listened.

"I think...I think most of her personalities are fake. I counted eighteen different personalities, but—"

Dr. Mansfield raised an eyebrow.

"Eighteen?"

Andrew nodded.

"Yes, eighteen. The old crone, the innocent four-year-old, the inquisitive seven-year-old, the bratty—"

Dr. Mansfield stopped him by raising a hand.

"Okay, fine, I know the personalities. Please, just go on with your diagnosis."

Andrew sighed.

"Like I was saying, I think that most of them are fabricated. In fact, I believe that all but two are just figments that she made up. But here's the thing, I think that both of these true personalities—which, incidentally, are the inquisitive four-year-old and the doting mother—*made up* the others. I need more time to tell which ones came up with which, but it's clear that both of her personalities are conjuring the others as a sort of coping mechanism."

Dr. Mansfield's brow furrowed. It was common for traumatic events to cause a person's brain to fragment, the result of which was often different personalities. It was something he had coined 'extreme cognizant dissidence'—a way of dealing with something that was difficult or impossible to comprehend.

He opened his mouth to say something, but then closed it again and observed Andrew carefully. The man, usually quiet, eyes downcast, was now staring him with an air of confidence that he hadn't seen before. And Dr. Mansfield found it slightly unnerving. And the diagnosis, while he had not come to the same conclusion, was interesting, to say the least. And advanced, if a little misguided.

"Alright, Andrew, let's say I buy your diagnosis. And, for the record, I too believe that the two main personalities are the mother and the seven-year-old. But now for the most important question." He paused for effect, and Andrew predictably leaned forward in his chair in anticipation. "Which is the real Giselle Stall?"

Andrew's eyes immediately narrowed.

It was a trick question, of course. There was no one 'real' Ms. Stall; Ms. Stall was all of her personalities, whether they were fabricated as Andrew believed, or existed in individual compartments of her mind.

Twice the man across from Dr. Mansfield opened his mouth as if to say something, but he shut it again. He sipped his coffee slowly as he waited patiently.

Eventually, Andrew answered.

"Both...and none, I guess. Giselle is both of them."

Dr. Mansfield nodded and finished the rest of his coffee. He placed the Styrofoam cup down on the table and was about to stand when Andrew spoke again.

"Did you see the scar on her chest? Right"—Andrew traced a finger from just below the hollow of his throat and drew a line partway down his breastbone—"here?"

Dr. Mansfield nodded.

"Yes, of course."

"It's from a lung transplant. When she was younger, very young, she developed severe pneumonia and her lung collapsed."

Dr. Mansfield's brow furrowed.

"And she received a transplant from—get this—a seven-year-old girl."

Andrew raised an eyebrow when he said this, as if it was an important revelation. Unfortunately, Dr. Mansfield wasn't making the connection.

"And?"

"And that's where her second personality comes from, Dr. Mansfield. It's from the transplant, and it's...it's...it's *someone else. There's someone inside her...*"

Dr. Mansfield immediately stood.

"That's enough for today, Andrew. You should go back to your room now."

Andrew rose and bowed his head again, the proud glint rubbed away from his eyes.

"Did I do something wrong?" he asked meekly.

"No, of course not. But you can't 'adopt' a personality from a lung transplant, Andrew. I think you know that."

Dr. Mansfield held the door open for Andrew to exit. But before he left, the man turned back.

"You can't?"

Dr. Mansfield frowned.

"No, of course not. Sometimes traumatic events, such as a serious illness, can…" Dr. Mansfield stopped himself before he started to ramble. "How did you know about Giselle's lung transplant?" he asked suddenly.

Andrew made a face as if Dr. Mansfield should know this already. Despite taking him along with him, George made a point never to show him the patient files, for confidentiality reasons, among others.

"Justine gave them to me, of course. Didn't she tell you?"

Dr. Mansfield's frown deepened and he made a mental note to speak to Justine when her shift started in an hour or so. It wasn't just that the nurse had shown him the files, which was definitely against the rules, but it was also the words that Andrew had used that perturbed him.

Of course—why of course?

"No, Andrew, she most definitely did not. Now please just head back to your room."

Chapter 5

SEAN SOMMERS TOOK A final drag from his cigarette before flicking it to the ground. Then he exhaled a thick cloud of smoke and stepped forward.

"Nice to see you, too," he said with a frown.

Robert's eyes narrowed.

"Can't say I feel the same."

Sean glanced over Robert's shoulder, his gaze leading to the Harlop Estate.

"No? You have me to thank for that house you have there."

Robert scoffed.

"You mean I have Ruth Harlop to thank for that."

Sean snickered.

"You think she signed that deed over to you? C'mon, Robert. I thought you were smarter than that. In fact, if that is what you truly believe, I should probably take this with me and just go."

Sean had one hand inside his navy peacoat and flashed the corner of an envelope before tucking it back in.

Robert suddenly had a change of heart. After all, he had a feeling that Sean knew more about the Marrow than all of the Internet sites he had frequented over the past couple of months combined.

Probably even more than LBlack, whoever the hell he was.

He reached out to grab Sean's arm, but the man pulled back.

"Wait—don't go. I have some questions..." His eyes were downcast now. "...some things I was hoping that you might be able to clear up for me."

Sean started to withdraw the envelope again.

"This is not Jeopardy, Robert. I'm not here to fulfill your desire to *know*. You need to come to grips with the fact that there are some things in this world and the other side that you will never be privy to." Sean pulled the envelope out of his pocket and held it out to Robert, much like he had all those months ago at his foreclosed home.

Just after Wendy died.

Robert felt an unexpected pang of sadness at the thought of his late wife. He had so entrenched himself in his research that he had had very little time to think about Wendy. Or Amy.

And perhaps that was the point.

But now, the reemergence of Sean Sommers brought back memories that he would have rather forgotten.

Like memories of Landon.

Fucking Landon.

"You want the job or not, Robert? Because—"

"What job?"

"Take the envelope."

Robert hesitated, but his curiosity grabbed hold and he accepted the envelope from Sean. He was apprehensive, of course, but a sudden surge of adventure coursed through him. And there was also the notion that Sean had answers...answers about the Marrow, among other things.

The fissure in the sky, the shrieks and the pain coming down like hail...

Robert used the flashlight from his cellphone to illuminate the printed document within.

Robert,

Pinedale Hospital has been closed for nearly a decade—abandoned. Until now.

A few nights ago, there was an awakening of sorts, and the Seventh Ward is now thriving, when it should remain silent. When it needs to remain silent.

We need you to go there and take care of this mess. In return for your services, you will receive $100,000.

Sean

Robert read the letter a second time, then a third. It was transactional, for sure, but he also noted some strange choices of words.

Like *we need you*, when the only name at the bottom was Sean's.

"What?" he asked, a smirk creeping onto his face. "No Uncle Tom or Aunt May to go and visit?"

Sean didn't smile. Instead, he pulled a cigarette from his pocket and lit it.

"This is not a game, Robert," Sean said after a drag. "No matter how much you or Cal or Shelly want to make it one. There is..." Sean let his sentence trail off, and Robert got the impression that the man had already said more than he'd wanted to.

"Go on," Robert encouraged him.

But Sean remained silent.

Robert put the letter back into the envelope and then tapped it against his palm for a moment.

Then he held it out to Sean.

"Thank you, but I'm not interested."

This time, a flash of emotion crossed Sean's face. He tried to hide it by taking another drag of his cigarette, but it stayed for just long enough for Robert to pick it up.

And in that moment, Robert knew he had the upper hand.

"This is not negotiable, Robert," Sean said flatly.

Robert shrugged.

"Look, you weren't there. You don't know how horrible it was to see little Patricia chewing on a goddamn rat, and that

psychopath James Harlop with the fucking flapping neck hole."
He waved a hand dismissively. "Not interested in seeing that
ever again, Sean. No thanks. I'll find another way to make some
cash, to stay afloat."

Sean eyed him suspiciously, and Robert thought for a second that the man might have figured out that he was being
played. After all, there really was no real way for them to make
any money, at least none that he hadn't already considered and
summarily dismissed. Still, Robert held his ground, staring into
the man's cold eyes, trying his best not to waver.

The old Robert Watts would have backed down, would have
walked away. But he wasn't the old Robert anymore.

Sean sighed.

"What do you want, Robert? One fifty? I can probably get
the price up to one fifty."

Robert shook his head emphatically.

"I don't want more money—I want answers."

His final word hung in the air like a foul smell. Sean seemed
to internalize this while he smoked the rest of the cigarette in
silence.

"One question," the man said at last, flicking the wasted butt
to the ground. "You send these ghosts back to where they be-
long and I'll answer one question."

Robert was like a child on Christmas morning. He could
barely contain himself.

"Great. One hundred grand and a question. It's a deal."

Robert held out his hand, but Sean just looked at it.

"How do I let you know when we are done?"

Sean's brow furrowed.

"I'll know—you just worry about the Seventh Ward."

The look sent a shiver up Robert's spine.

The Seventh Ward.

Unlike last time, he would make sure to get Shelly to look it up on the Internet to get a feel for what they were up against before rushing in like he had at the Harlop Estate.

"Will do," Robert said. After another awkward silence, he took this as his cue to leave, and turned with the intention of doing just that when Sean's voice brought him back.

"And Robert?"

"Yeah?"

"Don't even think about going back. You are to deal with the quiddity in the Seventh Ward, and that's it. Do you understand?"

Back... there was no need to clarify to *where* Sean was referring.

A sudden, pleasant warmth overcame Robert, and he felt his cheeks flush.

"Got it—I won't be going back," he lied.

Then he turned and made his way back to the Harlop Estate in a very different mood from the one he had left it in just a few minutes ago.

Chapter 6

FOURTEEN YEARS AGO

THE ODD CONVERSATION IN the lounge over coffee with Andrew Shaw signaled a change in the Seventh Ward and in Dr. Mansfield. The man's words had disturbed him, and while nothing Andrew had said or done was in and of itself dangerous, he decided to put the brakes on his special treatment. Andrew took the news surprisingly well, and it didn't even seem to bother him when word got around that Justine had been suspended for a week for sharing patient information. Seeing no further regression, Dr. Mansfield eventually started to trust Andrew again.

Andrew's strange behavior and odd comments constituted a momentary relapse triggered by direct questioning of a diagnosis that was similar to his own, he wrote in his case files. *Comments/actions not indicative of future behavior.*

Shortly after Justine returned from suspension, the Seventh Ward received six patients in a single week, including the incredibly difficult Mrs. Dupuis, who came with a delightful personality baggage of being a nymphomaniac. And as an 80-year-old malnourished, crass woman, she made everyone, including Dr. Mansfield, uncomfortable when this particular personality took over.

What was he to do? Just let the woman scream for hours on end while he tried to deal with Giselle and the other patients? Interviewing these patients, getting to the root of their problems, took time. Time he didn't have. Which was why he hadn't let Justine go after her egregious breach of protocol, and why he eventually brought Andrew back into the fold, despite not being fully comfortable with the idea. To mitigate the risk, this time Andrew was given specific instructions, in the rare case that he would be with the patients and Dr. Mansfield wasn't present:

1) He was in no way to attempt to treat the other patients;

2) The questions he was to ask were to be read directly from a script that Mansfield himself had prepared;

3) In no way was he to deviate from the script, irrespective of patient response;

4) He was to take detailed notes of patient responses in a notebook that he had been given.

It had been three days since he had hesitantly given Andrew this responsibility, and it was going better than he could have expected—both for him, in terms of lessening his workload, and for Andrew. Almost immediately, Dr. Mansfield saw a change in the man; he was returning to his more youthful, vibrant self—the way he had been before the incident in the lounge.

It didn't seem to bother the other patients, either; if anything, Dr. Mansfield had the general impression that they liked being interviewed by one of their own. Like they too could one day be like Andrew, part of a functioning, albeit highly structured 'society.' Some of them had even started calling Andrew 'Dr. Shaw.' which so long as Andrew wasn't the one to initiate, Dr. Mansfield didn't see a problem with.

Three days...for three days, this new scenario worked well.

But that all changed again when Dr. Mansfield lost his temper.

Normally even-tempered even during the most stressful of times, for some reason the caustic combination of lack of sleep and frustration eventually came to a head for Dr. Mansfield. The last thing he wanted to do was to shout at Andrew, especially given his history. But Mrs. Dupuis had been screaming for hours, and it was driving him insane. She had been given a hefty dose of Ativan the night before, and Dr. Mansfield still had to wait another few hours before he could sedate her again.

And for whatever reason, he just lost it.

"Fuck! Andrew, go take care of that woman!" he hissed, thrusting the manila envelope that he was holding at Justine. The woman dropped it, spilling papers all over the floor. For a second, Andrew just stood there, eying Justine as she bent to pick them up.

Dr. Mansfield resisted the urge to reach over and shake the man.

"Andrew, did you hear me? Go to the fucking room and take care of her! Make her shut up!"

Andrew's face became a deep crimson, and Dr. Mansfield instantly regretted raising his voice.

None of his patients responded well to threats or shouts. If anything, it only made their condition worse.

Dr. Mansfield shook his head and opened his mouth to apologize, but before he could get the words out, Andrew turned on his heels and quickly headed down the hall toward Mrs. Dupuis's room.

The man's gait had changed. It was slower, more deliberate. *Maybe this isn't such a good idea. Maybe—*

Justine distracted his thoughts by handing him the folder again. Dr. Mansfield stared at it for a moment, then peered up at Justine's doughy face.

"Sorry," he grumbled, turning back to Andrew.

The man was already gone.

Dr. Mansfield squinted down the hallway, wondering if maybe he had imagined the change in posture, the slowed gait.

I should check out the notes that he's been taking. And maybe it's about time I started paying a little more attention to his needs, and not so much my own.

Dr. Mansfield opened his mouth to ask Justine to retrieve the notepad when one of his other nurses suddenly appeared, her face flush.

"Betsy? What's wrong?"

The woman took a deep breath.

"It's Giselle. You should come quick—she's having another fit."

Dr. Mansfield swore under his breath, then thrust the folder back into Justine's open hands.

In the end, if he had just taken a moment to look at Andrew's notebook earlier, things would have been different.

Very different.

***

Giselle's fits ran the gamut from simple curses to extremely violent depending on who had control at that moment.

Betsy had been right to come get Dr. Mansfield; this was a bad one. It appeared as if a new personality had emerged, one that was just plain mean. Speaking in tongues, Giselle had waited until one of the orderlies had come in close to strap her down when she bit him. And it was no love bite, either; an apple-sized hunk of flesh hung from the man's arm.

The orderly, Vern, was a man that Dr. Mansfield had worked with for many years, so when he claimed that his hand shot out by accident, on impulse, he was prone to believe him. But Vern was a big man, a man who spent all of his time outside the ward in the gym. So when his hand had lashed out, it had shut Giselle up instantly.

Dr. Mansfield didn't think the young girl's jaw was broken, but it was still going to leave a nasty bruise. The Seventh Ward wasn't popular for visits—most of the friends and family of those that were admitted came for the first few weeks, months maybe, but with time, the frequency between them became longer and longer, until they inevitably stopped altogether. Especially if it appeared, from the outside, at least, that there was little improvement in their condition. It was just his luck that Giselle so happened to be one of the few patients that received regular visitations. Giselle's father, a partner in a medium-sized law firm, came for a supervised visit every Friday at exactly 11 AM. Only for twenty minutes, but still...today was Thursday.

Dr. Mansfield commissioned one of the nurses to tend to Vern's bite while he watched on, trying to figure out how he was going to deal with this scenario. With funding as tight as it was—requiring him to use a patient to perform the interviews—upsetting a patient's father, a lawyer, no less, was not going to help his bottom line.

He rubbed his fingers in his eyes, trying and failing to force away the fatigue that wrapped his very bones.

"Go home, Vern," he said with a sigh.

"Wha—why? It was an accident. Shit, I wouldn't punch a girl, you know that, Doc."

Dr. Mansfield, eyes still closed, nodded.

"I know, but you should still go home. Take an extended, long weekend."

The man chewed the inside of his lip before answering.

"With pay? Am I getting paid for this?"

Questions about pay reminded him of Andrew and Justine, and how the lack of funding had driven him to expand their responsibilities beyond what he should have.

Responsibilities...a patient seeing patients? Taking notes? What was I thinking?

But that was the thing; he *wasn't* thinking.

"Yeah, fine. Come back Monday," he said, finally opening his eyes. With a nod, Dr. Mansfield turned and left, heading directly for Andrew Shaw's room.

His eyes, dreary moments before, widened in surprise when he opened the door to find Justine sitting alone on the cot, her back to him.

"Justine? What are you doing in here?" he demanded. After her suspension, he had done his best to keep the two separated.

When there was no answer, Dr. Mansfield stepped into the small, eight-by-eight-foot room.

"Justine?" he asked again, raising his voice.

When she still didn't answer, he reached out and laid a hand on her shoulder.

"I'm talking to—"

Justine turned her head slowly, a strange expression on her pale face.

"He's onto something," she said slowly.

"What?" Dr. Mansfield's eyes darted to the notebook that lay open in her lap.

"I think Dr. Shaw knows how to fix these people."

Dr. Mansfield made a face.

"What the hell are you talking about? Give me—" He reached for the notepad, but she pulled it away from him.

"He can heal people," she hissed. "He *knows*!"

"Justine! Snap out of it!"

Dr. Mansfield aggressively reached around her thick body and wrenched the notebook from her hands.

"What's wrong with you?" he spat. "Take the rest of the day off, Justine. Think about—"

His eyes instinctively lowered to the open page of the note-book, and he immediately lost his train of thought.

What in the living hell?

Written on the top line was GISELLE STALL, in solid black letters. But the rest of the page, indeed, every single line contained the same sentence written over and over again in perfect cursive.

...there's someone inside me...there's someone inside me...there's someone inside me...

Dr. Mansfield whispered a curse, and then flipped to the next page. It was the same as the first, only with a different name at the top: MARGARET DUPUIS.

...there's someone inside me...

He quickly flipped to the next page, and then the next. The entire notebook was filled with the same insane sentence, repeated hundreds, if not thousands of times.

Dr. Mansfield was about to close the notebook, but he got to the last page and his heart suddenly skipped a beat.

The name at the top was his own: DR. GEORGE MANS-FIELD.

The lights in Andrew's room suddenly switched to red, and a piercing alarm suddenly filled the Seventh Ward.

"Shit," he swore, tossing the notepad onto the bed beside Justine.

Adrenaline flooded his system, momentarily displacing the feeling of dread and revulsion at the notebook that he had just read. Ignoring Justine, who was still staring at him, Dr. Mansfield rushed to the doorway, nearly crashing into an orderly that barreled in.

"Dr. Mansfield! Dr. Mansfield!"

The man doubled over, trying to catch his breath before continuing. His eyes were wide, his face pale.

"What? What is it?" he demanded. "What's going on?"

When the man continued his heavy breathing, and held up a hand to ask for a moment, Dr. Mansfield pushed by him and entered the hallway.

In all of his decade plus of working in the Seventh Ward, Dr. Mansfield had only heard the alarm go off three times. Once had been a false alarm, while the other two had been suicide attempts.

Only one had been successful.

Dr. Mansfield had promised himself that he would never let it happen again.

"It's Mrs. Dupuis," the orderly huffed from behind him. "Please, Doctor, you need to hurry!"

Dr. Mansfield immediately broke into a sprint.

Please...not again.

Chapter 7

ROBERT WAS SURPRISED THAT Shelly of all people was the one to object.

"No...no fuckin' way." Robert tried to get the letter back from her, but she pulled it away and leveled her green eyes at him. "The last time was the *last* time, remember?"

"The only time?" Cal offered.

Shelly shot him a look.

"I don't know what you are all excited about—you nearly crapped your pants when you saw Jacky. Imagine if it had been you in the basement dealing with James Harlop and not Robert? What then? We'd all be swallowed up and transported to his own personal hell by now."

Robert's thoughts went immediately to the feeling that had enveloped him as he stood on the soft shore of the Marrow, staring at the rolling waves. The way he had been so warm—not hot, but *fulfilled.*

If only they knew...

"Robert? What's wrong with you?" Shelly snapped, and Robert shook his head. He reached for the letter, and although she pulled back again, he managed to snag it from her.

"Look," he began, conscious that what he was about to say was going to come out patronizing, but unable to help it. "We need the money, Shelly—it's a hundred grand. Shit, with that money, we could live here for a couple of years...and with no worries about money, you and Cal can sit here and drink and bicker all you want."

Shelly growled.

"And what about you? You were shitting your pants too, scared of the fucking dark, if I must remind you. And now, what? You think you're a fucking bona fide Ghostbuster?" She threw her hands up and turned her back to him. "All this talk about money is great, fucking fantastic, but you get grabbed by one of these apparitions and get sent to the Marrow...you can't take your goddamn greenbacks with you there, Robert."

Robert reached out and laid a hand on her shoulder, and she whipped around, her eyes blazing into him.

He let his hand fall.

"Let's just check out the scene; if it's too much, we'll back out." He shook the letter. "We'll burn this letter and figure out some other way to make money." Robert indicated Cal with his chin. "Maybe Cal here can start stripping."

Shelly smirked, and he knew that her resolve was faltering. Cal must have noticed too, as he piped up.

"Fuck, if we have to resort to me stripping, we'll be drinking prison wine and not decades-old scotch, m'lady," he informed them, rubbing his round belly.

Robert reached out again, but this time when his hand fell on Shelly's shoulder, she lowered her gaze and didn't brush him away.

"We need you, Shelly. Cal and I can't do this alone. You know more about this stuff than both of us combined."

Robert waited, and eventually Shelly looked up at him. He was suddenly struck by how pretty she was, especially when she was being vulnerable, as she was now.

She pressed her lips together.

"Fine," she relented at last. "We go and check it out, but that's it."

Cal clapped his hands together in glee.

"Yippee! I'll go get Slimer and warm up the station wagon. Ectoplasm away!"

***

Robert laughed. He couldn't help it.

"What?" Cal snapped, his eyes narrowing.

"*What*? Seriously? What the hell are you wearing? You look like some sort of out-of-shape ninja."

Shelly joined in to his laughter.

"Like a—like some sort of swollen blood sausage," she added between laughs.

Cal looked down at his body, a frown on his face. While he was distracted, Robert stepped forward and flicked the black belt that hung from his waist.

"Where'd you get this, anyway? Is it a bathrobe or something?"

Cal shrugged and tightened the waist tie. He was sporting a black turtleneck, on top of which he wore a silky black bathrobe. He was also wearing a baseball cap pulled down low, and with his turtleneck pulled up high as it was, only his face was exposed. To top off the look, he was wearing a pair of cheap wool gloves.

"I dunno what it is...found it in a box in one of the back rooms. There are heaps of boxes that haven't been touched in years. Might be some gems or jewels in there."

Robert shook his head.

"Gems or jewels? Like a pirate's bounty? What the hell are you talking about?"

Cal raised an eyebrow.

"You never know."

"Fine, whatever, but why the fuck are you wearing that?" Shelly asked, hands on her hips. "I don't think I want to be seen with you...besides, it's best if you're alone when you get your big break. You know, when you're featured on *How To Catch A*

Predator. I can see the headline now: Rotund man in silky bath-robe seen handing out candies at the elementary school."

"Rotund? Fuck off. I just thought...I thought..."

Robert considered saving his friend, but he was enjoying Cal being embarrassed for once and not the other way around.

"Yes?"

"You know, about not touching and all that. I thought that if I wore this, maybe they couldn't get to my skin."

Robert chuckled.

"What? We don't know. Maybe they have to touch your skin."

Shelly made a face. The humor had suddenly left the room.

"Alright, whatever," she added, adjusting the backpack on her shoulder as she turned toward the door.

Robert hurried after her.

"What's in the bag, Shelly?"

"Tampons," Cal said quickly, pulling up the rear.

"Fuck off."

"Oh, sensitive, are we?"

Shelly ignored the comment.

"What *is* in the bag?" Robert asked again, genuinely curious.

She shrugged it off.

"Some stuff we might need." It was clear that she wasn't planning on expanding on this further, so Robert just let it go. Cal, on the other hand...

"Maxi pads?"

Shelly whipped around, and for a brief moment, Robert thought that she was going to reach out and hit him.

And he wouldn't have blamed her. Instead, she just smiled.

"Just take off the damn bathrobe, you perv."

Robert grinned, Cal frowned, and together the trio left the Harlop Estate.

Chapter 8

FOURTEEN YEARS AGO

IT WASN'T A SUICIDE attempt.

It was something much worse.

"Put down the scalpel, Andrew," Dr. Mansfield ordered calmly.

He barely recognized the man before him. Andrew Shaw's eyes were small and red. His hair, usually shaggy, was now a complete mess. Even his voice seemed different somehow.

"Call me Doctor Shaw, or I'll slit her throat."

Dr. Mansfield swallowed hard as he watched the man move the blade closer to Mrs. Dupuis's exposed neck. Andrew was crouched behind her as she lay on the gurney, completely nude. He looked out from over her right shoulder, one hand gripping the blade that was just now touching the leathery skin beneath her chin, while his other palm was pressed firmly against her forehead, pinning it to the gurney.

"Fine, fine, but please, just put the scalpel down. You don't want to do this."

"He ain't gonna do it," Mrs. Dupuis spat. "He's a fucking pussy—he don't have the balls to kill me."

Mrs. Dupuis had become the irate junkie, and Dr. Mansfield did his best to ignore her. Still, he knew he only had a little time before she was going to seize. Phantom personality or not, this version of Mrs. Dupuis still needed her drugs. And if she didn't get them, she was prone to quickly descend into violent convulsions.

And with that blade...

"Andrew—"

"*Doctor!*" the man suddenly screamed. "*Call me Doctor!*"

Dr. Mansfield held his hands up.

"Sorry, sorry. Doctor—Dr. Shaw—please let her go. We can talk about this."

Something flickered across Andrew's face, a representation of the man that Dr. Mansfield had first met upon entering the ward, the one that he had trusted enough to interview patients with him.

The man that he had taken pity on, most likely because of his medical background.

And also because he would be lying if he didn't see a lot of himself in Andrew Shaw.

Stupid…how could you possibly be so stupid?

"We can talk about it?" Andrew said with a sneer, the new version of himself, the one that Dr. Mansfield to this point had only read about, regaining control. He leaned out from behind the gurney and released Mrs. Dupuis's forehead.

"See? Told you this pussy can't do it."

Both men ignored the naked woman splayed on the gurney, and Andrew grabbed the neck of his t-shirt and yanked it down. "You want to talk about *this?*"

At first, Dr. Mansfield didn't know what Andrew was referring to, but when he leaned out even further, he caught sight of a thick pink scar that ran from the hollow of his throat before disappearing beneath his shirt.

His thoughts immediately turned to the comment that Andrew had made about Giselle's transplant and the words scrawled on every page of the notebook like some sort of demented mantra.

There's someone inside me…there's someone inside me…there's someone inside me…

"I was only twelve when they did this to me," he said, his voice dry and hoarse. "When they put someone else in here."

He retracted the blade from Mrs. Dupuis's neck for a moment to poke at the scar.

The woman immediately cackled.

"Told you! Told you! *Told you!*"

"But it wasn't until a couple of years later that I realized they didn't just put someone else in here" —he moved the scalpel to his hairline and used it to gently stroke his temple—"but that they put someone in *here*, too." Andrew lowered his voice until it was a mere whisper. *"There's someone inside me…"*

Dr. Mansfield took a small step forward, and Andrew immediately put the blade back to Mrs. Dupuis's throat. Her eyes suddenly went wide and immediately filled with tears.

"Please, please, Daddy, what's he doing to me? I don't want him to do this to me," she said between sobs.

The scared seven-year-old now. Dr. Mansfield shook his head, struggling to keep his focus despite the insanity that billowed about the room.

"Dr. Shaw, I know that you feel you have been wronged somehow, that your parents should have asked you if you wanted the transplant, but doing *this* is not going to make you any better. You know this," he said, trying desperately to appeal to the *other* Andrew Shaw. "You *know* this; and besides, you can't hurt anyone. You're a doctor, after all."

A smile started to cross Andrew's face, and Dr. Mansfield felt his heart sink. In that lecherous grin, he knew that his approach had failed. He immediately broke for the gurney, but despite his reaction, he was too slow.

"Oh, that's where you're wrong, Dr. Mansfield. I'm not a *real* doctor."

"Please, Daddy—"

Mrs. Dupuis's words regressed into a gurgle as Andrew drove the scalpel into the woman's throat all the way to the handle. Blood immediately sprayed from the wound, nearly reaching Dr. Mansfield, who was still four feet away.

"No!" he screamed, lunging for the gurney.

The demented man dragged the blade across her neck, making a thin red gash in her copper-colored flesh. The blood stopped spurting, and instead just flowed in thick rivulets, soaking the front of the old woman's neck, her sagging breasts. The sheet beneath her immediately turned a deep crimson.

Dr. Mansfield ran to her, his physician instincts taking over, any concept of danger to himself vanishing. Andrew stepped back as he neared, and Dr. Mansfield jammed his palms on Mrs. Dupuis's neck, trying to stem the blood that ebbed out of her. She was beginning to thrash, which only served to send more blood flying. It bubbled from her mouth now, and her eyes rolled back.

"Help!" Dr. Mansfield shouted, wondering why the orderlies and security were taking so long with the light and alarm flashing as they were. *"Help me! I need—"*

But then he felt something cold press up against his collarbone and he immediately stopped speaking.

"You don't believe me now, Dr. Mansfield—you don't believe that *there's someone inside me.* But you will. By the time I'm done with you, I swear you will. Together, we are going to make history."

Chapter 9

"PINEDALE HOSPITAL'S DOORS OFFICIALLY closed on February 25th, 2006, but the hospital had been in steady decline ever since the incident that occurred almost exactly five years prior."

Shelly paused and licked her lips.

"C'mon, why you stopping?" Cal asked.

Robert kept his eyes focused on the road ahead. He was only half listening to what Shelly was saying, despite a keen understanding that what she was reading was very important; that Pinedale Hospital was important, as was the Seventh Ward.

But he couldn't stop his mind from returning to Sean and the question he was going to ask him when this was all over.

And the Marrow; the Marrow was always on his mind.

"I'll wait for Captain Ghostbuster over here, make sure he wakes up from his wet dream first before I continue."

Should I ask him about what the lightning in the sky meant? Or what the water was? The sand? If I'll ever see Amy again? If I can go back, maybe?

The last thought made him shudder, but he wasn't sure if it was a manifestation of excitement or discomfort.

Or maybe it was a bit of both.

A hand suddenly smacked the back of his head.

"What the fuck, Cal?"

Robert shot the man a look in the rear-view, but Cal just stared back, shaking his head in disgust. Although their friendship had been strained from living together, as anyone's would, there was something different about him ever since they had purged the ghosts from Harlop Estate. He was, in a word, distant. Robert also thought he detected a hint of envy disguised in his biting satire.

There was no question that there was something building between Shelly and himself, and Robert knew that it was only natural that Cal, who had brought her into their fold, would be a little jealous.

Robert glanced over at Shelly, who was staring back at him. Her green eyes were wide, outlined by thick eyeliner that went beyond the lids and into a point—cat's eyes. This eyeliner was the only makeup she wore—that she ever wore—and yet her lips were always so red and juicy and—

"We're waiting on you, cowboy," Shelly said softly. As if knowing what he was thinking, her tongue snaked out and wet her lower lip. "What you thinking about, anyway? Still thinking about Wendy—"

"No, no," he interrupted, "nothing like that."

You wouldn't understand.

"I'm sorry, just tired, is all. Please, keep reading. I'm listening."

Cal grumbled something, but Robert didn't make out the words. A quick glance revealed that the man had crossed his arms over his chest and was now staring out the window, sulking like a petulant child.

Yeah, definitely envious. Not so disguised anymore, however.

Shelly gave him a look as if she didn't believe him, but continued anyway.

"Okay, so this fucking hospital? Pinedale? Shut down about a decade ago. But it was already on its way out because of an incident—"

"Yeah, we heard this shit," Cal said from the backseat, his eyes still trained out the window. "Get to the good part."

Shelly scrolled furiously on her cellphone.

"Alright, here we go… *On February 17th, 2001, nearly exactly five years to the day that Pinedale officially closed its doors, a patient from the Seventh Ward—the psychiatric ward—kidnapped the psy-chiatrist-in-chief, Dr. George Mansfield. The exact details of what happened on that fateful day were never released due to patient confi-dentiality rules, but over the years more and more information has leaked. What we do know was that there was an altercation of sorts involving a Seventh Ward nurse and two patients. When the dust cleared, one patient was dead and Dr. Mansfield was kidnapped by the other patient. The nurse also went missing, although it's still unclear if she was an accomplice or a victim. Believed to have escaped into the woods behind Pinedale, the police searched for days on end, but they came up empty. There was just no sign of the missing nurse, patient, or Dr. Mansfield. During the investigation, which is still open to this day, the Seventh Ward was temporarily closed, but it never reopened.*

"Two years ticked by without any progress, then three. Rumors started rumbling in Pinedale's other wards, with some patients claim-ing that they could hear Dr. Mansfield barking orders late at night when no one was around. It was during this time that the first body part was discovered: an amputated leg—from the knee down—was found in the bathroom in the Second Ward, jammed into a toilet. The next week, an arm was found in the sink of the women's bathroom in the Fourth Ward. DNA confirmed that both of these belonged to Dr. George Mansfield. As news of the man's dismemberment spread, peo-ple simply stopped coming to Pinedale, and soon the entire hospital was nearly as empty as the Seventh Ward. Which is why it came as no surprise that this past February, the Board of Directors decided that it was in the best interest of both their shareholders and the com-munity at large if Pinedale closed their doors for good. All patients were redirected to North Halichuck Hospital, a much newer facility, which is less than thirty miles north of where Pinedale is located. There are no current plans for the facility after the final patients are moved to NHH at this time. Although Dr. George Mansfield's entire body was never found, based on the dismembered limbs, his family and

the authorities have assumed him dead. The nurse and the patient are still officially considered missing."

A hush fell over the car as Shelly finished reading the final paragraph.

Then Cal said the word that was repeating in all three of their heads.

"Dismembered?"

Shelly shrugged, trying to remain tough, but even out of the corner of his eye, Robert could tell that she too was shaken.

"What it says... lemme..." she began playing with the phone again. "Lemme see what else I can dig up."

In the intervening minute, Robert felt Cal's hand up at his neck again, only now it was a gentle poke to get his attention and not a slap. Evidently, his sulking and staring out the window was over—for now.

Hearing about a man being dismembered would snap anyone out of a funk, he supposed.

"Did...what's his name, Steve? Did Steve tell you anything else about the Seventh Ward?" His words dripped with fear and apprehension.

Robert shook his head.

"It's Sean, and no. He didn't say anything about it, actually. I only know what you know—what was in the letter," he lied. Robert hadn't told them about the one question deal, but that wasn't for them anyway.

His thoughts drifted briefly to his last moments with Amy, when she had begged to hug him but he wouldn't let her. He had been frightened then, frightened at the idea of being pulled to the Marrow and not coming back, but now...just maybe, if the opportunity were to present itself again—

"Hey, Robbo, you spacing out again? What the fuck, man?"

"Sorry."

"I asked where you met Sean."

Robert shrugged.

"Look, I told you the story already. He came to my door with the letter from Aunt Ruth. Then I saw him again on my walk, smoking. That's it, man, really. I don't know anything about him. Maybe" — he hooked a chin at Shelly, who was still staring at her phone — "maybe after Shelly's done, she might be able to Google him. His name is Sean Sommers."

Shelly looked up at the mention of her name, and Robert was momentarily taken aback by how pale she had suddenly become. Even her lips had gone a shade of muted pink.

"Uh, guys, I think you are going to want to see this…"

Chapter 10

FOURTEEN YEARS AGO

"YOU COME NEAR ME, and I'll kill him. I'll kill him just like I killed Mrs. Dupuis," Andrew spat. He pressed the knife even harder against Dr. Mansfield's throat, drawing a thin line of blood.

There were three security guards and two orderlies blocking his path out of the room. All of the nurses that had initially rushed to Mrs. Dupuis's aid had since receded to their station, or were cordoned in the lounge, as was protocol.

All of them were safe, except for one. Dr. Mansfield caught a flash of the pale blue nurse scrubs between the three large security guards.

"Andrew," Vern began sternly. The man had obviously disregarded Dr. Mansfield's instructions to head home, and he was instantly grateful. After all, Vern was a big man. Very big and very strong. "Think about what you are doing—where are you going to go? There are police on the way—they'll be here any minute. There is no way that you will get out of here."

Andrew's eyes darted around nervously, and Dr. Mansfield felt the knife scrape up and down on his flesh as his hand jiggled.

"You hear that, George? They don't think that I'll be able to get out of here. What do you think?"

Dr. Mansfield swallowed hard. He had dealt with psychopaths before, of course, but he had never been in a situation like this…one that held such extreme consequences for himself. His mind whirred, trying to figure out the best approach—how he could save not only his own life, but save Andrew's as well.

After all, despite what he had done to Mrs. Dupuis, he deserved help.

He was sick, and all sick people deserved a chance at getting healthy again.

"Eh, George? What d'you think?" Andrew's hands were covered in blood, and when he spoke, his wrists stuck uncomfortably to Dr. Mansfield's neck.

"I think—I think that you can end this, Dr. Shaw. End it now."

"Oh? End it?" He pushed the blade just a little harder, "End it like this?"

"No!" one of the orderlies shouted.

"Please," Dr. Mansfield pleaded, immediately changing tactics. His hope was to try and bring the Andrew he had met to the fore again, but with the blade cutting into his skin, he couldn't concentrate. "You don't have to do this. I can help you, I know—"

Andrew laughed.

"You can help *me*? See, that's where you have it all wrong, George. You can't help me—*I* can help *you*. I know how to fix these people. You, on the other hand—"

Another voice entered the fray, one that belonged to the woman in the blue nurse scrubs.

"He's right," Justine said just loudly enough to be heard over the alarm that continued to wail. "He can actually help these people. Don't you want that? Doesn't everyone here want that?"

Dr. Mansfield's eyes narrowed and he felt the pressure on his neck ease just a little.

"Justine? What the hell are you doing?" he demanded.

The woman raised her eyes to stare at him.

"I'm helping the good doctor," she replied instantly. "Didn't you read the notebook?"

Dr. Mansfield was incredulous, recalling the single line repeated over and over.

...there's someone inside me...

"It was nonsense, Justine. The scribblings of a very, very sick man. You can't—"

She frowned and shook her head.

"Come with me, Andrew. I know a way out...a way out back and into the hills, somewhere you can slip out."

The knife was back against his Adam's apple again.

Justine's eyes went wide with excitement.

"Come, come," she said, shoving one of the security guards to one side and waving both Andrew and Dr. Mansfield forward.

"You try anything," Andrew whispered through clenched teeth, "and I won't hesitate to cut him open."

With the blade digging into his skin, Dr. Mansfield had no choice but to step forward when Andrew nudged him in the back.

At first, everyone remained rooted, unsure of how to react. But then Andrew shouted, and they instinctively made a path.

"You hear that? Get the *fuck* out of the way!"

Vern made eye contact with Dr. Mansfield, waiting for an indication, any suggestion—a nod, a wink, a fucking swallow—to pounce. But George Mansfield was a psychiatrist, not a hero.

He lowered his gaze and shuffled forward again.

It was the last time he saw Vern, or any of them, ever again.

***

"Where are you taking me?" Dr. Mansfield gasped.

The blade was still pressed tightly to his throat, and with every uneven step they took up the side of the hill, it jostled, scraping like the straight razor of a barber suffering from Parkinson's.

"You'll see," Andrew said, shoving the doctor forward once more. "You'll *see*."

Before leaving the hospital, Justine had secured some length of cable and had wrapped it around Dr. Mansfield's hands in front of him. The terrain was difficult enough—steep, and overgrown—but without his hands to balance himself, he found himself stumbling every four or five steps.

His knees were raw and chafed beneath his pants and lab coat.

The police have to be coming soon, don't they?

He perked his ears, trying to pick up the sound of sirens, but the only thing he could hear was the sound of the alarm coming from the smashed window somewhere behind and below them.

"Move," Andrew ordered, and Dr. Mansfield picked up the pace to avoid being shoved again.

Security? Will security come after us?

Justine, whose face was beet red, and who was desperately trying to catch her breath, finally appeared in his periphery.

"Justine," Dr. Mansfield begged. "Don't do this. You're a good person, I know that. Whatever you think—whatever you think that Andrew is going to do for—"

Something hard suddenly struck the base of his skull, and stars flashed in front of his eyes. He cried out and fell forward, smashing his chin and elbows on the terrain in front of him.

Groaning at the dull throb that seemed to encase his entire head, he struggled to roll over, but couldn't manage with his hands bound. Instead, he craned his neck around, trying to figure out what had happened.

Andrew Shaw was hovering over him, a leer on his face and a blazing look in his eyes. In that moment, Dr. Mansfield knew that this man would do anything to prove his insane theory.

He just hadn't yet figured out what role he had to play in all of this.

...there is someone inside me...

As darkness started to overtake him, Dr. Mansfield's gaze slowly drifted down to Andrew's left hand. In it, he held a fist-sized stone streaked with blood.

His blood.

"I told you already," Andrew hissed. "You are to address me as Dr. Shaw. After all, I am about to make the greatest psychiatric discovery in the last fifty years."

Dr. Mansfield's eyelids dropped, and then they closed completely.

"And you, George Mansfield, are going to help me."

Chapter 11

ROBERT SWALLOWED HARD. HIS stomach and constitution had hardened after seeing what he had in the Harlop Estate, including James Harlop's gaping neck wound.

But this was different. The images on Shelly's phone were not of ghosts, apparitions, or quiddity, but of real body parts. Bloody, ragged stumps.

"Fuck, put it away," he grumbled, bringing his eyes back to the road.

"Sick," Cal added.

"What? Now you guys are becoming pussies? When I was the one that said this whole fucking thing was a bad idea, you guys were quick to tell me otherwise. But now when there's a little blood involved, you guys are suddenly squeamish?"

Shelly paused, but neither Robert nor Cal offered a response.

"Look, you guys need to smarten up. I may not have been in this game for long, but I've been around it for more than both of you combined. And what the fuck? How am I the one that has to be rational? Jesus, you guys didn't look up the Harlop Estate on the 'net, and now a man offers you some cash—"

"—a hundred grand—"

"—fuck, whatever, some guy offers you a shitload of money, and you think all you're going to have to do is wave your pretty asses in the air, toss a gas mask or book at a ghost, and then poof, we're rich? You think this is the newest installment of Paranormal Activity? Paranormal Activity: Indecent Proposal Edition?"

Robert glanced back at Cal in his silk robe and felt a smile creep onto his face despite Shelly's tone.

"It's not a joke, Robert. We got lucky last time…really lucky. In fact, I can barely believe that you made it out of the basement at all. This...this is different. This time, we are in a foreign place—a fucking hospital, of all things—and we have no idea what's waiting for us inside. Seriously, you think that these limbs are bad? I have read—I've read—"

"Shelly, we aren't taking this as a joke," Cal interrupted her, his tone soft, soothing.

Shelly rolled her eyes.

"Don't patronize me. This is going to be fucked up, Cal. More fucked up than the Harlop Estate. I just hope that you are ready for what is to come."

Cal shrugged.

"I have no idea what to expect, but if there's one thing..."

When he paused, Robert's gaze flicked up to the rear-view mirror. Cal had that same look on his face, the one that he had first seen when his friend had spoken about the train accident, when he had watched his friend die. Back then, Robert had thought that there was more to the story, but at the time he hadn't pressed. A pang of guilt unexpectedly struck him.

In the three months since that they had lived together, it hadn't even crossed his mind to ask Cal about the incident. He had just been too wrapped up in his own shit. In the Marrow.

Fuck.

Shelly spoke next, but this time her tone, like Cal's, had become subdued. There was also something foreboding in the air, a feeling that had first arisen when Shelly had read those fateful words.

Dismembered.

Robert shuddered.

"I just want you guys to take this seriously. This is...this is no joke. We can enter this hospital, this *Seventh Ward*, and never come back out again. And the place that the quiddity might take us...well, there ain't no leprechauns and rainbows there, let me tell you."

Cal cleared his throat.

"We said we'll take a look. If it's too fucked up, we walk away. That's all there is to it."

All three of them nodded and then the car fell into silence.

"Guys?" Robert said after several minutes.

"Yeah?"

Robert pulled the car to the faded lift-arm gate and stopped.

"We're here. Behold, Pinedale Hospital in all its glory."

No one in the car laughed.

They didn't even smile.

***

The first obstacle was the gate, which was so worn and weak that it basically crumbled when Cal tried to lift it. The second proved more formidable.

"You sure your boyfriend didn't slip a key into the envelope?" Shelly asked, her trademark humor slowly creeping back.

"No, just the letter," Robert replied with a shrug.

Shelly reached up and yanked ineffectively on the thick metal padlock that kept the front door firmly shut. There was another lock closer to the handle, a smaller but more rugged-looking hunk of metal, and this was also locked.

Shelly shrugged.

"That's it, then. Let's go home, then, boys," she said, only half serious.

Cal stepped forward, and Robert smirked at his sudden chivalrous behavior. The man's feelings for Shelly ran deeper than he had first thought.

"Lemme try."

Shelly stepped aside.

"Be my guest, Sir Gallahad."

Robert watched on in amusement, ready to step forward and stop the man from hurting himself. That is, until Cal reached into the back of his silk bathrobe and pulled out a full-sized crowbar.

Robert's eyes bulged.

"What the shit? Where the hell did you get that from?"

Cal chuckled as he started to wedge the crowbar between the lock and the metal door.

"You think I'm only good at digging graves, Robbo?" he grunted as he applied force to the lever. It didn't budge. "I'm also—" He wheezed and applied more pressure. "—excellent at—"

Robert could see a vein in his forehead start to throb. The lock, however, was ambivalent to his exertion. With a violent shove, the crowbar slipped and Cal jammed his hand against the door.

"Shit..." he said, sucking the small cut on his finger and putting the crowbar back to wherever he'd gotten it from beneath his robe. "Won't budge."

Shelly laughed.

"What? You got something in that Hello Kitty backpack that you think you can do better with?"

"I have a blowtorch in here, but I don't think it'll do much to that lock."

Robert gawked.

"You *what*? You have a blowtorch? Jesus Christ, am I the only one that didn't come armed with a machine shop?"

"Stop bickering and let's find another way in," Shelly said.

Robert still felt a little naked, given that the only thing that he had brought with him was the letter that Sean had handed him. And of course the small, square photograph of Amy.

He brought that with him everywhere, either jammed into his wallet or just in his pocket.

"Fine, but you're leading the way with your crowbar, Cal."

Set with the back side butting up against a large hill, Pinedale Hospital reminded Robert a lot of the Harlop Estate. It didn't have the same pedigree, of course, as it was less than sixty years old, but it looked worse for wear. There was graffiti everywhere; graffiti covering older graffiti, making all of the tagging nonsensical smears. It was like Jackson Pollack had been commissioned to paint over the Mona Lisa.

Pinedale wasn't a particularly large hospital, which wasn't much of a surprise given that the town of Corgin only boasted a population of seventy-five thousand. Robert's eyes instinctively flicked upward, and he counted the windows that were covered with wire mesh.

Seven floors… the top floor must be the Seventh Ward.

Cal suggested that they stay out of sight given that it was still early afternoon and it would not go over well if they were confronted armed with a blowtorch and a crowbar.

No, Officer, we weren't trying to break into the abandoned hospital. We were just starting a machine shop in the parking lot.

Robert would take low odds on talking their way out of that one.

The trio snaked their way around the side of the building, then hurried through an abandoned parking lot.

"I think we have to go the other way," Cal offered when they reached the corner of the building, which pressed up against the side of the hill. Up close, the hill was far steeper than Robert had first thought. Although he could see the top, he had no idea what was beyond the thicket of trees that sprouted from the apex.

Robert pushed by Cal to get a better look around the corner of the hospital. While there were trees on the top of the hill, the vegetation on the actual slope, and behind the hospital, was fairly sparse. It also seemed to open up a bit just a few feet in— there was at least a foot of separation between the outer wall and the hill.

"Pass me your cell, Cal," he demanded. Even though it was still sunny out, the hill blocked most of the natural light.

Cal handed over his phone, the flashlight already on. Robert took it, and then leaned around the corner of the building and shone the light back there. For a second, the only thing he saw was more overgrown weeds.

"You see anything?" Cal asked, his tone suddenly more mellow than it had been when he'd been tackling the front door.

"Naw, I think we can fit through, but—" Robert waved the cellphone back and forth. "—wait a sec. I think there's a window back here." He switched off the phone and eyed Cal. "Looks like we can *probably* fit through."

Cal snorted.

"Fuck off, I'll fit."

Robert went first, then Shelly. True to his word, with a little awkward yoga and rhythmic sucking in and out of his gut, Cal managed to squeeze between the wall and the side of the hill. The effort reddened his face, and sweat had formed on his brow; Robert guessed that this was the second most exercise that the man had gotten in years.

The first being digging the graves for the Harlop family, of course.

As Robert had suspected, it opened up a few feet behind the hospital, and after a few seconds they could comfortably walk single file. Soon Robert found his gaze drifting up the embankment to their left.

Is this how the crazed patient escaped the hospital with the doctor?

From this angle, the trees at the top looked massive, giant spires heading into the stratosphere. Still, he couldn't imagine how the police could never find them.

"Robbo, pay attention," Cal snapped.

The light from the cell had drifted with his gaze, and he immediately focused the weak beam on the grass in front of him.

As they approached the window, the light started scattering off something in the overgrown grass: shards of glass.

"Looks like we weren't the first ones to come back here," Robert grumbled, shining the light at the smashed window for them all to see. The opening measured at least two feet by two feet—more than large enough for them all to climb through.

"We can fit," Robert confirmed as he inspected the sill. There was something dark on the edge, something that instinctively reminded him of blood. He considered running his fingers across the smudge, but decided against it. He kept this to himself, raising the light above it.

"Hey, Cal?" he asked, his eyes now trained on the dark interior of the hospital. The feeble light cast the old-fashioned black and white linoleum tiles in an eerie blue glow.

"What?"

"It's your last chance."

"For what?"

"To take off that ridiculous outfit."

Shelly laughed. Robert was in the process of turning to glimpse the expression on his friend's face when movement from inside the hospital caught his eye.

"Fuck off, Ro—"

"Wait!" Robert gasped. "There's something in here!"

Chapter 12

DR. MANSFIELD SLOWLY STARTED to regain consciousness. His head hurt, his eyes hurt, and his wrists hurt.

His neck was chafed and raw.

At first, he had no recollection of where he was.

Did I go out after work? Have a few too many drinks with one of the pretty nurses?

An image of Betsy, the newest nurse intern, young blonde, perfect breasts, in her bright blue scrubs flashed in his mind. But as he blinked several more times, he realized that the face he was seeing wasn't a memory, but that it was actually real. Slowly, however, Betsy's smooth, caramel-colored skin started to become paler, and then it started to widen.

"No," he murmured as Justine leaned in even closer.

He tried to move away from her, but his arms and legs were locked in place and he couldn't budge. Snippets of what had happened, of finding Andrew Shaw's notepad, of Mrs. Dupuis bleeding out on her bed, and the trek up the hill behind Pinedale with the scalpel pressed to his throat came flooding back.

Tears welled in his eyes.

"Where—where am I?" he asked, his throat dry, his voice hoarse.

While his arms and legs were bound to some sort of wooden table, spread out at his sides, he was free to lift and move his neck around. It appeared as if he was in some sort of cabin with dull brown walls and a single window off to his right.

It was completely black outside.

Nighttime…how long was I out? And where the hell are the police?

"He's waking," Justine said softly, but Dr. Mansfield ignored her. Instead, he whipped his head around again, trying to take in as much of his surroundings as possible before Andrew did anything else to him.

The smell of vegetation—moss, maybe, or wet leaves—filled his nose.

Yes, a cabin in the woods…I must be in some sort of cabin or hunting lodge.

He couldn't locate a sink or toilet in the cramped, eight-by-ten-foot space, only a bucket and some sort of repurposed ceramic basin.

Short-term stays…fishing cabin, maybe?

"Dr. Shaw?" Justine said, drawing his gaze back.

The nurse was staring directly ahead, over Dr. Mansfield's head. Tilting his throat toward the ceiling, he could just barely make out the outline of a figure hovering over him. There was a lamp or light of some sort—*no sink, no electricity, most likely*—behind the figure, basking his features in shadows. But when the light glinted off a scalpel blade, Dr. Mansfield, if he had any doubts before, knew exactly who it was.

"Yes," Andrew Shaw replied softly, "I can see that."

The man moved what Dr. Mansfield now saw to be a lamp off to one side, bathing the left side of his face in a strange, orange-yellow glow.

"Welcome back, George."

Dr. Mansfield swallowed hard.

"What—what are you going to do to me?" he asked, a tremor in his voice. His head hurt, and speaking only made the pain worse.

But he had to convince Andrew to let him go. Worst-case scenario, he had to stall. Stall long enough for the police to rescue him.

Andrew chewed his lip as he contemplated an answer, during which Dr. Mansfield listened for the sound of sirens, or better still, the sound of people outside the cabin. He wasn't local to Corgin where Pinedale was located—he lived closer to the much larger North Halichuck—but as an avid walker, he spent many a lunch hour out behind the hospital, wandering through the very woods that he assumed he was in now.

There had been many occasions in which he had had to use his GPS watch to find his way back. The original plan, as the rumor went, was to develop the area behind the hospital, build up Corgin into a bustling metropolis. To date, however, this had become something of a pipe dream. The builders claimed that it was just too expensive, that cutting down the trees and flattening the rock outcroppings would stretch them too thin. Dr. Mansfield suspected that the very verbal outcry from environmentalists was the main reason that nothing ever got moving. On other days, this didn't bother him. If anything, it made his daily walks more enjoyable. In this moment, however, lying nude, his wrists and ankles bound by what looked like extension cords, he wished that they had fucking clearcut the damn thing.

Turned it into a goddamn parking lot.

"I'm going to prove to you, Dr. Mansfield, that *there is someone inside me.*"

The man stared at Dr. Mansfield expectantly.

He wouldn't give Andrew the satisfaction he so richly demanded.

"Andr—" He caught himself. "—Dr. Shaw, what you are saying—that you have a disorder, someone else trapped in your head because of a transplant you received when you were young—it's just baseless. It's not...not true. It can't be true. Please, you need to let me go. I can help you, Dr. Shaw. But I can't—" He strained against his wrist restraints. "—I can't help you here. Not like this. Please, you need to let me go."

Dr. Shaw hesitated, his face beginning to go slack. For a moment, Dr. Mansfield was struck with the notion that the other version of Andrew, the one that he had brought with him on patient interviews, was about to return.

But then Andrew's eyes went dark again.

"How long have you been working in the Seventh Ward, Dr. Mansfield?"

"Sixteen years."

He didn't like the question; something told him that it was all leading up to a conclusion, one that he wanted no part of.

Fucking cops—where are you?

"And how many people have you helped? How many have you cured?"

Dr. Mansfield shrugged as best he could, given his position on the table.

"Hundreds."

Andrew's lips pressed together tightly, and he shook his head. The scalpel came into view again, only this time it wasn't held up like a spear, but pointed directly at his chest.

"Wrong answer," he said flatly. Then he turned to Justine. "Get undressed," he ordered.

Justine's eyes went wide, and for a second Dr. Mansfield thought that Andrew had pushed her too far, that whatever he was planning was just too out there for her. But to his horror, the nurse didn't hesitate; she slipped the scrubs down over her shoulders and allowed them to pool on the floor.

Her massive white breasts sagged nearly to her navel, the nipples as big and round as apples.

Dr. Mansfield looked away, tears spilling down his cheeks now.

"You are going to actually be part of something...of something real special, Dr. Mansfield."

The scalpel lowered and Dr. Mansfield cried out as he struggled against his restraints.

"Justine, don't let him do this! Please! This is crazy! Get him—"

"You are finally going to help cure people, Dr. Mansfield," Dr. Andrew Shaw whispered as he lowered the scalpel to the doctor's bare chest. "There is someone inside me, and soon there will be someone inside you."

He plunged the scalpel into his skin and Dr. Mansfield started to scream.

**

"Wha—what did you do to me?" Dr. Mansfield stuttered. His words sounded strange to him—warbling and tainted, with an odd inflection.

He attempted to look around, but one of his eyes was dark, and the vision in his other one was clouded.

"Hello!" he shouted. "Dr. Shaw! What the hell did you do to me?"

A groan from his left suddenly drew his attention. His head instinctively whipped that way, but it was his bad eye and he couldn't see much. With his right eye, he could make out that he was still in the cabin, and that it was still dark out, but not much more than that.

A bout of dizziness suddenly struck him, and he nearly panicked as he teetered on the verge of passing out. He closed his eyes and tried to take a few deep breaths to avoid succumbing to the panic that welled inside him. But halfway through his first breath, he felt an unnatural clicking sensation in his chest, followed by what felt like fluid seeping into his body cavity.

What the fuck?

"He's filling with blood," he heard someone say. It was Dr. Shaw's voice, or he thought it was, but something was wrong with his ears as well. Underlying the voice, he could hear what sounded like rushing water or coursing blood.

A thump in his chest, and his heart started to flutter.

I'm dying.

"Justine! Get the coagulant over here! We're losing him!"

Dr. Mansfield's good eye fluttered, and he turned to face the general direction of the voice. It was then that he saw the thick, oblong object lying near the ceramic basin. It was fizzing slightly, the surface covered in a layer of tiny bubbles, and he knew exactly what it was.

It was his lung.

Hands were suddenly on his chest, a dull pressure that felt strangely comforting. His vision continued to flicker, his mind wavering. He thought about Betsy and some of the other nurses that he had brought through the Seventh Ward in his time.

Peaceful, serene thoughts; good thoughts.

He didn't think about Mrs. Dupuis or Dr. Shaw, even when the man started shouting at Justine, screaming that his heart was failing, that he was seizing.

A small smile crept onto Dr. Mansfield's face as he felt what was left of his vision fading to black, and time seemed to slow.

"We've lost him," he heard Dr. Shaw mutter, his voice filled with dismay.

There was a long pause, and when Justine spoke next, it sounded like she was speaking underwater, and he could barely make out the words.

"What do we do with him now?"

A contemptuous sigh.

"We still have lots of him left...and someone else will come around. Dr. Mansfield will still be part of this discovery. Smile, Justine, our work is not done yet. Not by a long shot."

Chapter 13

"You sure?" Shelly whispered. She had crept up behind him and was now pressed against his back, trying to get a better view of the inside of the hospital.

"I'm—I dunno," Robert replied. He was *pretty* sure that he had seen some movement down the end of the hallway, but when he had looked again, he only saw shadows.

For nearly a minute, he resigned himself to just slowly swinging the cellphone flashlight back and forth trying to identify anything that might have moved.

"Hold on a sec," Shelly said, peeling herself off of Robert. She squatted and removed her backpack before reaching inside. Then she pulled out two massive metal flashlights.

"Blowtorch and flashlights? You're just full of surprises, ain't ya?" Cal said. Shelly ignored him and handed one to Robert and reserved one for herself. "Oh, yeah, figures. I'll just light the way with my fucking crowbar."

Shelly hushed him, and Robert quickly handed Cal back his cellphone. Then he turned his attention to the broken window, aiming the flashlight inside before clicking it on.

"Fuck," he swore, immediately recoiling and shielding his eyes. "Where the hell did you get these from?"

Unlike the cellphone, the flashlight was incredibly powerful, seeming to fill the entire hospital with artificial light.

"Army surplus," Shelly replied, her voiced tinged with pride.

Squinting hard while his eyes adjusted, Robert turned back to the hospital. The window was near the center of a long hallway, the opposite side of which was punctuated by several plain doors placed at regular intervals; patient rooms, he assumed. The entire place was covered in dust—the floor, the walls, the small desk off to Robert's right.

If he had seen something, it must have either been flying or gliding over the floor, as none of the thick layer of dust seemed to be disturbed.

He swallowed hard.

A thought of something gliding over the floor might have previously been met with a chuckle, but the idea of someone—*Jacky Harlop*—gliding across a floor—*mud, her golden hair perfect, the rain seeming to fall around her*—no longer seemed humorous.

At both ends of the hallway were identical, solid-looking doors.

Robert angled the flashlight upward slightly, and picked up red lettering on a gray sign that hung from the ceiling.

First Ward, it read, then beneath that, *Outpatient Clinics.*

He turned back to the others.

"Can't see anything...doesn't seem that anyone has been in there for years. Everything is covered in dust."

Cal looked around, eyeing the thick vegetation on the side of the hill, then brought his gaze back to the broken window.

"No tracks of any kind? Animals? Birds even?"

Robert shook his head.

"Well, then," Shelly interjected, "what are we waiting for? Let's go inside."

Despite her words, she didn't move.

"So you go from not wanting to even come here to being eager to go inside?" Cal asked.

"For a hundred fucking grand, I'll at least take a look in an abandoned hospital, thank you very much," she snapped back. "Besides, I had to spend two hours in the car with you smelly fucks—need some *fresh* air."

Still, despite their bickering, neither made a move toward the window. Eventually, Robert took the lead, which was only fitting, given it was he who had received the letter from Sean.

And he was also the one who was desperate to have his questions answered.

"Let's do this, then," he said, trying but failing to instill his voice with confidence.

Robert cautiously swung one leg over the windowsill, and then the other.

The fall was higher than he had expected, and he landed with an *oomph* and his knees locked uncomfortably. A cloud of dust swirled up to greet him, and he coughed while ineffectively trying to swat it away.

"It's clear," he said, turning back to the window. He reached up to help Shelly through the opening, but she shooed him away.

Her landing was more graceful than his, but she still stirred up nearly as much dust as he had. They both started to cough.

"You got any gas masks in there?" Robert asked, blinking rapidly, trying to clear his eyes.

"Yep," Shelly replied, and at first Robert thought that she was joking. But when she dug out three white painter's masks, he scoffed.

"For real? Jesus, what else do you have in there?"

"Tampons," she said with a sly grin, before bringing the mask up to her nose and mouth. Robert was also smiling when he put his mask on.

Shelly was right, of course; none of this was a joke or to be taken lightly. But for some reason, Robert suddenly felt *alive* for the first time since Amy had died. He was no longer attached to his computer, and with the added element of danger...it all made his blood pump in a way that it hadn't in months.

And it felt *damn* good.

Cal came through the window next, and in typical Cal style, he did so loudly. A grunt, a couple of curse words, and he was finally inside. He brushed the dust off his shirt, then eyed the mask that Shelly held out to him.

"Really?"

Shelly nodded, and Cal slipped his mask on.

For a moment, they all stood there in the center of the hallway, Shelly and Robert splaying their flashlights in either direction, Cal with his hands on his hips looking like a unionized ninja taking his requisite break. For all of their pep talks in the car, and Shelly's warnings, they hadn't actually come up with much of a plan.

Back in the Harlop Estate, they had bound the Harlop family to items that they had found about the house, based on what they knew of them. But here? In Pinedale Hospital? They had no idea who they were going to encounter, let alone what these people held dear. Robert assumed that there was a doctor here, one that had been murdered, dismembered even, but it was a hospital…who knew how many dead they might encounter.

"So?" he asked tentatively, trying to stem his runaway thoughts. His voice was muffled by the mask. "Where to now?"

Shelly shrugged.

"The letter said the Seventh Ward, right?"

Robert nodded, and Shelly turned the flashlight up to the sign that he had seen earlier.

First Ward: Outpatient Clinics.

"I guess that means we go up, then, doesn't it?"

They went left down the hallway, only because there was an image of a staircase above the door at the end. As they walked, slowly, trying their best not to stir up any more dust, Robert began to ruminate over how foolish they were actually being.

Cal, evidently, was thinking the same thing, as he asked the question that was on Robert's tongue.

"So what do we do when we find them? I mean, we have to bind them, right? Rebury them, like the Harlops?"

Shelly, who was leading the way, stopped so suddenly that Robert nearly crashed into her back. She didn't turn when she spoke next.

"You ask this now?"

Cal shrugged.

"Well...yeah. I mean, what the fuck are we going to do?"

Shelly made a noise that Robert thought might have been a sigh, but it was difficult to tell beneath her mask. Then she started moving again. They reached the door and she slammed both hands against the bar, filling the entire ward with an echoing clang.

"Jesus, Shel," Robert said.

This time she turned.

"What, you think we are going to wake the dead? Sorry to break it to you, Robert, but they're already awake."

With that, she stepped into the stairwell, and both Robert and Cal followed.

Like the outpatient ward, the stairway was equally dusty and untouched.

Robert shone his flashlight upward to the winding metal staircase above. He could see the door to the second ward, and the third, distinguishable only by the large numbers painted in red on their matte gray surface.

Shelly didn't hesitate; she immediately started upward.

"I say we observe first," Robert offered. "We wait and watch. If we see the doctor—what was his name? Gainsfield?"

"Mansfield," Shelly corrected him.

"If we see Dr. Mansfield, we can try to talk to him first. Remember what you guys said about Jacky and Amy? About how they were just confused? Maybe the quiddity will be the same here. Maybe the doctor might just want to be released—to go on his way. We might even be able to ask him where his body is."

Cal, huffing now into his mask, spoke next.

"You mean his body parts?"

"What?"

"He was dismembered, remember?"

Fuck.

Robert had forgotten about that. And all his talk of the doctor was deliberately avoiding mention of the patient that had done the dismembering.

What were they supposed to do with him? Have a nice little chitchat? Some tea, perhaps?

Robert shook his head, trying to clear the pervasive negativity that blanketed his thoughts.

"Shel, do you think we have to bury all of the body parts? Or just—"

"I'd be more worried about the patient, if I were you," she said flatly.

"The patient?" Cal asked, his voice wavering.

Robert swallowed hard, and even his best efforts couldn't shake the unnerving feeling that washed over him.

Shelly stopped suddenly and turned, looking past Robert to Cal, whose eyes were red and watery from all the dust.

"Yeah, you know? The one that did the dism—"

But another voice, this time neither Robert's, Cal's, or Shelly's, filled the stairwell, and all three of them stopped cold.

"Where you guys going?"

It was a woman's voice, and it was coming from somewhere below them.

Robert, eyes wide, turned to Shelly, but she offered no support. Her gaze was locked on a spot below them, trying to see who had spoken.

"Hello?" the voice asked again.

For some reason, this query snapped Cal out of his stupor and he actually answered.

"H—h—hello? Is someone there?"

Robert's brow furrowed.

So much for just waiting and watching.

A woman's pale, round face suddenly poked from around the lower level of the staircase.

"Hi," she said, smiling widely. "You're here to see the doctor, right?"

Robert felt himself nodding despite himself, and his hand instinctively went to the picture of Amy in his front pocket. It offered him comfort to know that she was here with him, even if it was only in the form of a passport photo.

"Well, Dr. Shaw is waiting for you. He's down here in the Seventh Ward."

Robert swallowed hard, and Shelly unexpectedly reached out and grabbed his arm. He nearly jumped, but this did nothing to lighten her grip.

Her fingers bit into his skin, sending pain shooting up and down his forearm.

Dr. Shaw? Who the fuck *is Dr. Shaw?*

The woman's blonde head ducked out of view, and they listened as she receded down several stairs.

Robert immediately thought of the dust that blanketed the floor in the First Ward. Either this woman hadn't been up there in a while—how long? Years, maybe?—or she had found another way in.

Or...

"Well? Are you coming? The doctor's been waiting for you."

Shelly's fingers bit even deeper into Robert's forearm, and a sudden sense of dread washed over him.

...or this woman that is luring us into the basement isn't alive.

PART II - Surgical Intervention

Chapter 14

NINE YEARS AGO

THE WOMAN WATCHED FROM the trees, her dark eyes peering out from between the spindly trunks. It was nearing midnight, and the moon cast the hospital in thin streams of bluish light.

There was only one car in the parking lot, a champagne-colored sedan with rust clinging to the wheel wells. She watched in silence, waiting. After five minutes, the door to the hospital squealed and opened. A squat man in khakis and a polo stepped out, the moonlight reflecting off his bald head. He held the door open for a few seconds, peering down the hallway almost longingly. Then he closed the door, which sealed with a metallic thump.

The man retrieved a padlock from his pocket, and flipped the metal bracket across the door and locked it in place. Even from her vantage point high above, the woman could see that the lock was hefty, solid. And yet even when he affixed a second, smaller lock further down, near the handle, a smile crept onto her face.

After testing to make sure that the door wouldn't budge, the man reached up and scratched at his bald head. Hands jammed in his pockets, he eventually turned and walked toward his car.

Although he opened the car door immediately, he hesitated before stepping inside, his gaze drifting upward.

The woman didn't move, but for a split second she thought that their eyes met. But then the man looked away and got into his car.

She watched him drive away, the smile on her face growing from a grin to one of Cheshire proportions.

The man hadn't seen her.

No one had.

It had been five years, and in that time, they had forgotten all about her. Her and *him*.

But they would soon remember.

The time for watching and waiting had come and gone. The time for acting had returned.

The woman pushed herself to her feet, brushing the leaves from her body, all the while keeping her eyes locked on Pinedale Hospital.

It's time to wake the doctor, she thought as she headed back into the forest. *It's time to wake the doctor and get back to work.*

It's been far too long.

Chapter 15

ROBERT APPREHENSIVELY FOLLOWED THE strange woman with shoulder-length blonde hair in the nurse scrubs, ready to turn around and bolt should she make any sudden movements. He could hear Cal's heavy breathing directly behind him, and behind Cal, he thought he could hear Shelly, too.

Naturally, his first thought was that she was an apparition—one of the trapped quiddity. But having followed her for more than a minute now, he was no longer so sure. For one, her scrubs were blue…faded, granted, but definitely blue, whereas everything that James and Patty Harlop had worn was a washed-out gray. Even their skin had had a sickly pallor.

But Amy…Amy seemed so real, her shirt so pink.

Robert's head began to throb, and he found himself receding into the dark place he had so desperately clawed out of only a few months prior. A place of confusion, where things didn't make sense, but had distinct, and severe, consequences.

"Please," the woman said over her shoulder. "Through here."

The nurse, who had now reached the basement level, used a keycard to activate the magnetic reader to the right of a heavy metal door.

The resultant beep cut through the fog that encased Robert's mind, and two things suddenly became clear: one, that he somehow needed to get his hands on that card; and two, that there was a speck of blood on the otherwise gleaming white ID card.

When she yanked the door wide and held it open for them, Robert stopped on the third rung of the stairs. He tried his best to observe the woman, squinting, tilting his head, looking for something, anything, that would help him ascertain if she was a real person or a ghost.

The problem was, he had no foolproof method of determining if she was real.

Except one, but *that* was out of the question.

He tried angling the flashlight, trying to see *through* the plump woman, but there was just too much dust in the air and it blurred his vision.

Besides, both Ruth and Amy had seemed so *solid*.

He made a mental note to look for a solution to this problem on the Internet when they got back to the estate.

Maybe to ask LBlack or Sean about it.

The nurse pursed her lips together in a thin smile.

"Oh, c'mon. He's waiting for you."

Shelly cleared her throat, and it was all Robert could do not to turn and face her—he wasn't going to take his eyes off the mysterious nurse.

"You said—uh, you said a Doctor...*Shaw?*"

The woman nodded vigorously.

"Yeah, that's right. Dr. Shaw. He's been waiting."

"You sure you don't mean Dr. Mansfield?"

Something dark passed over her face, and for a brief second Robert thought he saw her eyes darken, threatening to become dark pits. But when he blinked they were back to normal.

"Oh, Dr. Mansfield is here somewhere, too. But he's not in charge anymore. That's Dr. Shaw. He's the chief now."

She leaned forward suddenly, and Robert recoiled, an action that only made the nurse's smile grow.

"Want a tip? He only likes to be called Doctor," she giggled. "Made the mistake of calling him Andrew once; won't be doing that again, let me tell you."

The nurse waved a hand over the threshold.

"C'mon, now. Go on in. Don't want to get the doctor angry. Normally we have this whole patient check-in thing—" She lowered her voice. "A waste of time, if you ask me, but one of the other patients has been acting up, lately, and he's been keeping Dr. Shaw busy for a while now. So, please..."

Patients? She thinks we're patients?

Robert stole a quick look at Cal and then Shelly. The expressions on their faces matched his own: confused, suspicious, and of course, scared.

He shrugged and took the initiative.

They'd made it this far, and besides, although the woman was strange, she didn't seem that dangerous.

"Okay," he said softly. The final few stairs suddenly seemed incredibly steep, and he was reminded of his fall into the Harlop basement.

This time, however, he had a flashlight and made it to the landing without falling. His eyes darted to the keycard reader and he noted a small green light in the upper right-hand corner.

Is there power here? Or does it run on some sort of long-lasting batteries?

Something to consider, in case the flashlight donked.

Robert swallowed hard as he neared the woman, his heart starting to race. As a last-ditch effort to determine if she was real, he shined the light directly at her, and her pupils dilated.

The nurse shielded her face with her arm.

"Sorry," he grumbled, lowering the beam.

She certainly *seemed* real enough. Still, before he was within arm's length of her, Robert gestured with an open palm toward the doorway.

"After you," he said with a weak grin.

"Oh, a gentleman, are you? Well ain't that nice."

She stepped over the threshold, and Robert waited for her to pass through before he grabbed the door. It was heavy, and he had to plant his feet to stop it from closing.

"And after you," he grumbled, indicating for Cal and Shelly to follow. Cal took his sweet ass time, his forward momentum hampered by the fact that his right hand was tucked behind him. Although it snaked up under his ridiculous robe, Robert would have bet all hundred grand that his meaty hand was gripping the crowbar.

A lot of good that'll do if she is a ghost.

Shelly went next, her eyes locking on Robert's as she passed.

Robert couldn't hold her gaze. It was an accusing look, a look that said, *you got us into this mess.* One that said, *if it looks fucked, we'll leave? Isn't that what we agreed? What, this isn't fucked enough?*

With a deep breath, Robert stepped into the long hallway, which was indistinguishable from the First Ward up above.

He took two steps and the door closed behind him with a loud click.

Robert jumped. He whipped his head around, and the breath caught in his throat at the sight of the large red seven painted on the back of the door.

Then the nurse spoke again, and he abruptly turned forward.

She was walking backward now, her hands out at her sides as if in celebration.

"Welcome, my newest patients of the Seventh Ward!" she exclaimed with a hint of glee in her voice.

Chapter 16

NINE YEARS AGO

DR. ANDREW SHAW TOOK a deep breath and closed his eyes, trying to focus. When he opened them again, the scalpel in his right hand had stopped shaking. It had been a long time since he had performed any sort of surgery, a long time since he had been back in his hospital.

"Nurse, wipe my brow, please," he instructed. The nurse used gauze to soak up some of his perspiration.

"Thank you."

Dr. Shaw turned his attention back to the man on the gurney.

It didn't matter how long he had been away. This discovery was too important to be hampered by his trepidation.

The man was completely naked; only his genitals were covered with a blue cloth. He had an oxygen mask strapped on his face, obscuring his features, and a blood pressure monitor on his finger. Off to the left was the O2 machine and the digital tracing of his heart rate on screen. It was slow, even: 120/83.

Perfect.

"Okay, Justine, you remember the plan, right? The surgical plan we went over?"

The woman, a doughy creature who was as short as she was wide, nodded, the soft skin beneath her chin quivering madly.

"Yes."

"Repeat it back to me."

The woman's eyes went wide, and she looked frightened.

"Oh, oh, okay. First you are going to make an incision just over the left, uh, left, uh shin—"

"The medial muscles, and then the tibia," Dr. Shaw corrected her.

"Ah, yes, the medial muscles and tibia, and then you are go-ing to—"

The man on the gurney stirred. His head shifted, just a little, no more than an inch or two, but it was enough for Dr. Shaw to notice.

"Okay, never mind that. I'm going to remove his leg and hand it to you, okay? After I get through the soft tissue, I need you to pass the bone saw. It'll get messy then, but you need to stay calm. He should—" Dr. Shaw checked his watch quickly. It read half past three. "—he should be out for another two hours. Should be enough time. I'm going to pass you the leg, and you put it on ice immediately, okay? Then we are going to take it to the other room while he's recovering. Then it's time to get his brother, okay?"

The nurse nodded eagerly, and Dr. Shaw sighed.

"Justine, you can't *fuck* this up."

Justine stopped smiling.

"No, Doctor. I'll remember."

Dr. Shaw's expression softened.

"Good. Now let's get started."

***

It took more than the two hours Dr. Shaw had planned.

The problem was the bone saw. It was old, and wasn't nearly as sharp as he had hoped. Halfway through the man's tibia, it snagged and stalled. When he tried to start it up again, it binded and he couldn't get it loose.

The man on the gurney moaned into his mask, which fogged over.

"Shit," Dr. Shaw swore. "Justine, we need to hurry! Grab the other saw."

Justine, her face a mixture of fear and anxiety, just stared at him.

"Fuck! Justine, get the goddamn saw!"

Dr. Shaw tried to turn the bone saw back on again, but the blade was completely jammed in the bone and it refused to move. The motor started to smoke.

"Over there! The one with the wooden handle!" he shouted, jabbing a finger toward the hacksaw on the metal table with all the other tools.

Justine finally snapped to and rushed across the room, her wide hips bumping into the heart rate monitor, sending it rolling away. As if in response to the nudge, the man's tracing suddenly increased in pitch.

"Hurry, Justine! He's waking! Fucking *move!*"

Justine increased her waddling speed. She grabbed the saw and brought it over to Dr. Shaw, whose eyes remained locked on the man on the gurney. His cheeks were pinched, creasing forming by the outer corners of his eyes; the drugs were wearing off, but he couldn't give him any more. They were a precious commodity, and he needed to save what little he had left for the man's brother.

Dr. Shaw snatched the saw from Justine's doughy hands and instructed her to get up next to him.

"I'm going to try and wedge this blade between the electrical saw and the bone, and when I say, give the bone saw a yank. Once it's out, I'll push this one in and then hack it off manually."

Justine nodded again, the strange grin returning to her face.

"We have to hurry, though…this isn't going to be pleasant, especially with him waking."

Dr. Shaw, grimacing, checked the surgical ligatures on both sides of the man's knee. They were still tight, which was good.

One slip, and the man would bleed out, and they only had three units of fresh blood left. He glanced quickly at Justine, sizing her up as she stared at the man on the gurney. His gaze drifted to her fat arms that seemed to ooze out of her scrubs.

Five years in the woods, living off berries and sparse game meat—squirrels, rats, the occasional rabbit—and she hadn't seemed to have lost a pound.

That's good…Justine has a strong constitution. She's also a universal donor O-; if push comes to shove, and I need blood…

Dr. Shaw shook his head and leaned over the gurney. He pressed the hacksaw up next to the other blade, wincing at the sound it made as it skipped across the exposed bone.

"Okay? You ready?" he asked, twisting the blade ever so slightly.

Justine nodded eagerly.

"On three: one…two…three!"

On three, Justine pulled. At first nothing happened; the blade was just buried too deep.

"Justine! Pull! *Fucking pull and lift!*"

Justine obliged, pulling with all of her substantial girth.

There was a terribly coarse tearing sound, and the blade finally slid out. Justine stumbled backward when it released, knocking the monitor over completely and falling on her ass. She cried out, but Dr. Shaw ignored her.

Acting immediately, he forced the hacksaw into the existing groove, then started to move it back and forth, slowly at first, trying to get into a rhythm.

But then the man on the gurney groaned and his eyes fluttered.

"Shit," Dr. Shaw swore. There was no time for precision.

In one smooth motion, he hoisted himself onto the gurney, straddling the man's legs. And then, more like a logger than a doctor, Andrew leaned into the sawing motion, running the entire length of the blade back and forth over the man's tibia with as much vigor as he could muster.

Grunting with the effort, sweat pouring from his forehead, Dr. Shaw failed to notice when the man's eyes snapped open. He didn't even notice when the man's other leg, the one not being amputated, started to twitch. What drew his attention was the man's hand that clumsily banged into the back of his arm as he furiously pumped the saw back and forth.

His first thought was that it was Justine, but a quick glance over his shoulder revealed that the fat nurse was still struggling to get to her feet like some sort of obese, overturned tortoise.

Then he noticed the man's hand.

"Shit! Nurse! *Nurse!* Hold him down!"

Justine finally made it to her feet and she hurried over. With both hands, she grabbed the man's arm and pressed all of her weight on top of it. She applied so much pressure that the man fully awoke, and he immediately started screaming into his oxygen mask.

Even though the words were garbled, muffled, Dr. Shaw knew what they were.

"What are you doing to me?" the man shouted. Then he let out a horrific, ear-piercing scream.

Thankfully, despite being fully conscious now, the sedatives still had a hold on part of his body.

A man as large and muscular as this one would have tossed Dr. Shaw off him like a ragdoll if he regained full control of his faculties.

Just one more… just one more…

But it took more than one; it took seven more strokes before the hacksaw suddenly made it all the way through the tibia. Dr. Shaw, arms and shoulders aching, gave a few more strokes to cut through the much smaller fibula, then quickly pulled the man's leg free of his body and held it high above his head like some sort of grotesque, organic trophy.

Then he wiped the sweat from his face with his shoulder and hopped off the gurney.

When the man caught sight of what was in Dr. Shaw's hands, his screams reached a fever pitch. And then, unbelievably, he started to sit up.

Dr. Shaw jammed the limb into the ice bucket and then ran to the door to the operating room. Nurse Justine tried to follow, but the man had regained enough use of his hand to reach up and grab a handful of her dry, blonde hair. Her eyes bulged and she shouted something, but with the adrenaline pumping in his ears, Dr. Shaw couldn't make out the words.

He used the keycard on his hip to open the door, then pulled it wide, turning back one final time.

Justine was trying to smack the man's hands away, but he was too strong. There was no way that she would be able to fight him off, especially with the way his thick fingers were wrapped and twisted in her hair.

It was too bad; Dr. Shaw needed the help.

But Justine surprised him by yanking with her neck, and a huge clump of her hair and some of her scalp peeled away. A moment later, she was standing beside him again, and together they stepped out of the room, allowing the door to quickly close behind them, beeping as it locked.

Justine brought a hand to the back of her head as she watched the man. When she pulled it away, her fingers were red with blood, but this did nothing to knock the grin off her face.

"Let's go," Dr. Shaw ordered. "There is more work to do tonight. Much more work."

Chapter 17

THEY WALKED THREE ABREAST down the hallway, keeping a good six or seven feet between them and the woman who had introduced herself as Nurse Justine.

"Listen, uh, Justine?" Cal asked hesitantly. His hand was still locked on the crowbar tucked beneath his bathrobe.

"Yes?" she replied without turning.

With every step, her hair shifted a bit, and Robert noticed that there was a patch missing at the back. An area that she had tried, but failed, to completely cover by brushing.

"I think you might have us confused with someone else. We aren't patients of the Seventh Ward."

Justine stopped and the trio immediately followed suit. Then she slowly turned to face them.

"You sure about that? I mean, if you aren't patients, then what exactly are you doing here?"

Robert glanced quickly to Shelly, but she just shrugged. He opened his mouth to say something, but took his time, hoping that Cal would interject. After all, he was the one who had started this dialogue.

"Ah, I'm just messing with you. I know why you're here," she said with a grin.

Alive or dead, there was something very wrong with this woman.

"You do?" Robert asked, eyebrows raised.

"Yes, of course." She squinted one eye and then aimed a finger at Cal. "You are…Cal." She pointed to Shelly next. "You're Shelly." She stopped at Robert, her smile growing. "And, of course, you're Robert Watts."

Robert gaped.

It was a setup; that bastard Sean set us up to be trapped here with this psychopath.

Justine laughed.

"Like I told you, the doc—"

"Who told you our names?" Robert demanded, his throat suddenly incredibly dry. When she didn't answer, and instead swiveled on her heels and started to waddle away, they stood their ground.

"Hey!" Shelly suddenly shouted. "How'd you know our names? Did Sean tell you?"

Justine stopped, but didn't turn this time.

"Sean? Don't know a Sean. It was Leland who told me."

"Leland?" Cal asked, his voice but a whisper. "Who the fuck is Leland?"

Justine sighed.

"Leland Black..." When none of them responded to the name, Justine sighed. "You might know him better as the Goat, though."

Robert's blood suddenly turned into ice in his veins.

A flash of James Harlop, the poker embedded in his skull, reaching down and grasping his hands flashed in his mind.

Your wife is here...so is the Goat. And he's coming...

"Goat?" Cal asked, shaking his head. He looked around. "Last time I checked, this ain't Old Mc-fucking-Donald's farm here. What the *fuck* are you talking about?"

Cal turned to Robert for support.

"Shit! Robert? You okay?"

Robert still couldn't move, haunted by the words that James Harlop had first said, and Justine had repeated.

It's a setup. It has to be.

Justine spoke up.

"You should ask Robert about the Goat, he'll tell ya."

Now it was Shelly's turn to interrupt.

"What the hell is she talking about, Robert?"

When Robert just continued to gape, fear coursing through his every capillary, she elbowed him hard in the side and he finally snapped out of it.

"Robbo? What the fuck is she talking about?"

"It's just—" He struggled to get the words out. "It's just—I dunno, it's just something that James Harlop said to me before—"

He caught himself before saying, *before he took me to the Marrow.*

"—before I bound him to the fireplace poker."

Shelly squinted, a clear indication that she wasn't buying his story. But before she could press him, the nurse whistled.

"Come on now. You can share stories some other time—we don't want to be late. Like I said, the doctor has one hell of a temper."

Robert exchanged a look with Shelly, who shook her head.

"We aren't going anywhere. Tell this doctor...this Dr. Shaw, if he wants to see us, he's going to have to come here."

Justine's expression didn't falter as she turned and approached one of the several identical doors that lined the inner hallway. She used her keycard to unlock it, then held it open expectantly.

"As I said, Dr. Shaw is busy with one of the other patients. He'll be ready for you soon, though. Please step inside your room."

Justine had an unnerving smile on her face, a look that made Robert squirm.

Something is very, very wrong with this woman.

"I think...you're off your fucking rocker if you think we are going into that cell," Cal said. In his periphery, Robert saw the hand behind his back start to move, threatening to pull out the crowbar. Robert grabbed his shoulder, staying him.

The last thing he wanted to see was this portly nurse bludgeoned to death in the Seventh Ward, no matter how weird she was. That would just give them another ghost to purge.

If she was alive, that is—and Robert still wasn't certain either way.

A howl, a dry, aching sound that was only remotely human, suddenly filled the entire hallway. Robert instinctively cowered, his grip tightening on Cal's shoulder. Shelly slid next to him.

"What in God's name was that?" Robert whispered breathlessly.

"I warned you, Dr. Shaw is with a patient now. But he'll be done soon. And he won't be happy if you aren't in your cell."

Robert, still trembling from the roar, replied quickly, "And I told you, we aren't going in there."

Shelly laughed again.

"It's not for *you*—the three of you—it's just for *you*, Robert."

"Fuck this," Cal whispered. "No amount of money is worth all this craziness. Let's get the fuck out of here."

Shelly made a face, as if to say, *I fucking told you this was going to be messed up. That it wasn't a joke, or a game.*

"I'm not—"

At long last, the grin on Justine's face faded. It was replaced with something akin to sadness.

"Please, there's someone in there that wants to see you. She says she missed you."

Robert's heart began to race again.

"Wha—who?" He took an unconscious step forward, his hand snaking into his front pocket, fingering the picture therein.

Even before Justine replied, however, Robert knew the answer.

"Your daughter, silly. Amy's in there."

Robert immediately moved toward the door. In the back of his mind, he knew that this was a mistake, probably just a trick, but he was helpless to stop himself.

He *had* seen Amy after death, and with what little they knew about the Marrow, maybe it was possible that she *could* come back.

And what he wouldn't give to see her again.

No matter how unlikely this scenario, the possibility was enough to propel him forward.

Cal grabbed the back of his arm, but he shrugged the man off.

"It's a trick, Robbo. Stay here!"

But Robert's rational mind had abandoned him.

Still keeping his distance from Justine, he peered into the room. But as he splayed the beam of light into the room, the flashlight suddenly flickered and went out.

Just as the lights had done in the Harlop house all those months ago.

His heart skipped a beat, remembering what Shelly had said about the strange relationship between the quiddity and lights.

Maybe she is here.

"Robert! Robert, get back here!"

Robert turned, but time had slowed, and he suddenly felt dizzy.

Shelly and Cal were sprinting toward him, but despite their alarm, something in the back of his mind told him that he should go inside the room.

That he *had* to go in the room, for Amy's sake.

"Go inside, the doctor's almost ready for you," Justine said gently.

Now on the threshold of the room, Robert turned his back to his friends. The flashlight blinked on again, only for a second, illuminating the beige walls. Squinting against the bright light, he caught sight of a small pink-and-purple bunny rabbit propped up on a wooden chair in the corner.

"Mr. Gregorius!" he shouted.

He ran for it, but when he squeezed its soft stomach, a stark realization hit him.

It wasn't Mr. Gregorius; it was just a plain, dollar store stuffed rabbit.

Robert turned toward the door just in time to hear the lock engage. It beeped once, and then Justine's face filled the small rectangular glass window.

She was smiling again, and like in the basement of the Harlop Estate, Robert was once again alone.

Chapter 18

<u>NINE YEARS AGO</u>

A LOUD THUMP FROM one of the other rooms distracted Dr. Andrew Shaw and his hand slipped, driving the suture too deep into the man's leg.

"Fucking hell," he murmured from between clenched teeth. He used his shoulder to wipe away a bead of sweat before it fell into his eye, and then pulled the thick suture out of the man's skin and reset it. He was just about to loop it again when the thump hammered the wall again.

"Fuck, Justine, you wanna do something about that?" He cranked his neck to look at the doughy woman, who was hovering predictably over his shoulder. "Justine?"

"Huh, what?" she asked, her grin becoming a startled expression.

Dr. Shaw pressed his lips together tightly, trying to keep his emotions in check. It would do him no good to fly off the handle, especially while Justine still held some value.

"The noise. Go make the man stop thumping on the wall."

Justine just stared at him for a moment as if trying to decipher his words. It wasn't the first time she had acted this way; sometimes her mind just seemed to lock up even with the simplest of instructions.

He tied off the suture, then put the needle down on the gurney and surveyed his work. It wasn't perfect—far from it—and the fact that the man's twin had awoken during the amputation hadn't helped any. As it was, Andrew thought that this leg was a little shorter than the other, but it would have to do.

With a heavy sigh, he turned back to Justine, who was still standing there expectantly.

"Just go over there. Make him stop so that I can concentrate. I don't care how you do it. *Just make him stop.*"

The nurse finally seemed to understand and she swiveled on her heels, a sloppy, uncoordinated movement, and then went to the door. Before she pulled it wide, however, Dr. Shaw spoke again.

"Shut him up. I'll be over there soon…almost done here."

Justine nodded and then left the room, leaving Dr. Shaw alone with his current patient.

For the tools that I have? Not too shabby. Not too shabby at all.

The skin tone didn't quite match—the lower half was a little darker than the upper—which was odd considering that the donor was his twin. Maybe one had just come back from vacation?

Dr. Shaw shook his head.

Aesthetics didn't matter. What mattered was proving his theory. Proving Dr. Mansfield wrong.

His chest suddenly started to itch, and he used his gloved hand to scratch at the thick pink scar that ran from his throat nearly to his navel.

There's someone in here with me.

Those had been Andrew's words, not Dr. Shaw's, but they held so much meaning, so much power.

A smile crossed Dr. Shaw's lips as he thought back to the last time that Andrew had surfaced, nearly five years ago.

That had been a productive day, as not only had Andrew been buried, but it was also the first time he had killed.

His eyes clouded over as he remembered…

"Fuck! Andrew, go take care of that woman!" Dr. Mansfield shouted.

Something inside him clicked, just like it had after the transplant and after his attendant had screamed at him. He could feel the other person inside him start to rise, to bubble to the surface.

Andrew walked slowly, trying to keep the other at bay, to remain in control. It was a constant struggle, because he was there—Dr. Shaw was always there...watching...waiting for just the right moment to rise up.

The lights in Mrs. Dupius's room were off, which was strange, as the patients never had control of their own lights. Andrew's hand found the switch, but when he flicked it up and down, the room remained dark.

What the fuck?

By squinting hard, he could just barely make out Mrs. Dupuis's outline on the bed. Her sheets had been balled up and tossed on the floor, and her hands were off to her sides, suggesting that she was asleep.

Wasn't she just screaming? Was it her? Could it have been someone else?

Andrew wondered if perhaps sheer exhaustion from her near constant fits over the past few days had finally taken over. With this in mind, he moved closer to the bed, while at the same time looking about the room as his eyes slowly adjusted to the darkness.

He was nearly beside the plain wooden bed when he realized that Mrs. Dupuis was completely naked.

Holy—

Embarrassed, Andrew looked away, his face immediately reddening. He was about to turn and leave the room, to let one of the nurses know that Mrs. Dupuis needed dressing, when she moved, drawing his eyes back.

The elderly woman was staring directly at him, her eyes wide, somehow bright despite the dim lighting.

"Jesus," he gasped, startled by the sudden movement. He was about to move away, when her hand darted out with speed that belied her age. Before he could react, her fingers locked onto his balls and squeezed.

He cried out, but she squeezed even harder, stopping the sound before it could leave his throat.

"I want you to fuck me," she demanded, her voice nearly sinister. "I want you to fuck me *hard*."

Andrew swallowed, and his eyes moved down her eighty-year-old nude body, Dr. Mansfield's words echoing in his head.

Go to the fucking room and take care of her!

Confusion started to pass over him in waves.

Dr. Mansfield couldn't have meant that, *could he?*

Mrs. Dupuis's tongue darted out of her mouth and flapped rapidly, her eyes seeming to grow even larger.

Andrew's eyes moved about the room, trying to find inspiration or answers in something, anything. But as his gaze passed the square window over the door, he spotted the nurse's cart. There was a reflective object on top, sticking half out of a blue bedpan.

Take care of her!

Dr. Mansfield's words echoed in his head.

Mrs. Dupuis's gnarled hand squeezed even harder, and he started to feel nauseous.

And that's when the *other*—Dr. Shaw—made his play.

"No," Andrew croaked, but it was too late.

"Yes," Mrs. Dupuis replied. "Oh, yes."

The man in the scrubs made a *tsk, tsk, tsk* sound out of the corner of his mouth, his eyes still locked on the nurse's cart.

Looks like someone left a scalpel out. That's a no-no. Don't the nurses know that these patients are dangerous?

His eyes whipped back to Mrs. Dupuis's prone, wrinkled form.

"Oh, I'll fuck you alright," Dr. Shaw said, his eyes twinkling. "And you're going to love it."

The man on the gurney moaned softly, drawing Dr. Shaw out of his reverie. He shook his head and wiped more sweat from his brow.

I'm close, he thought, staring at the man's grafted limb. *This time it will work. This time you'll see. This time he will start acting differently, taking on his brother's personality. You'll see. I wasn't always like this.*

His scar began to itch again, but this time he resisted the urge to scratch.

There is someone in here with me...but he won't be taking control anytime soon.

Chapter 19

"OPEN THE FUCKING DOOR. I'm warning you, lady, you don't want to fuck with me."

Cal was holding the crowbar out in front of him aggressively, but his hands were obviously trembling.

Justine didn't move, didn't even acknowledge his order.

"Did you hear me? I said, let him out of there. *Now.*"

Shelly had moved next to him, and he could feel her heart beating even though they were still several inches apart. It was causing her entire body to rock back and forth.

There was still no response; ever since the overweight nurse had turned away from the window of Robert's room, she had said nothing. And yet, she was still smiling.

Cal took a step forward, raising the crowbar up even higher, making sure that even if the bitch was short-sighted she would see it now.

"I'm going to give you—"

A horrible roar, the same guttural, throaty growl, interrupted him.

Cal cringed and instinctively brought the crowbar closer to his body. Shelly was directly behind him now, her arms wrapping tightly around him. He tried to be brave, to be strong, but his hands were shaking so violently that the crowbar had become a blur.

What the fuck was that? And what in God's name are we doing here?

But he knew what they were doing here...or, more specifically, what *he* was doing here.

For years, Cal had done his best to forget that feeling...the feeling that had coursed through him as he held his seven-year-old friend as he died, the boy's blood soaking his arms and legs.

How could he explain the feeling of absolute euphoria as his best friend's quiddity left him? Better yet, how could he explain seeking this same feeling for over a decade? One that he could never quite replicate?

One that he had nearly forgotten about before Robert had begged him to come up to the Harlop Estate. On that day, it had all come flooding back.

Which was the *real* reason why he was here, in this place, the Seventh Ward, with a demented nurse, Robert locked in a cell, and promises to meet an undoubtedly cheery Dr. Shaw.

Another growl ripped through the hallway.

And that...there was that, too, whatever the fuck it was.

Cal shuddered.

"That's George," Justine said, as if reading his thoughts.

"Who the fuck is George?" Shelly spat.

The door at the far end of the hallway behind Justine suddenly burst open, banging loudly against the opposite wall. The nurse immediately stepped to one side as a hulking beast stepped through the opening.

"F-f-f-uck," Cal moaned.

Shelly was still clinging to him, but he stumbled backward anyway, nearly knocking her over in the process.

The man was gigantic, nearly seven feet tall and thick through the chest and arms. But despite his impressive musculature, there was something slightly off about him. It was as if Cal was looking at the man's reflection in a mirror that had been shattered: his face didn't quite line up right, one leg looked longer than the other, and one forearm was only about half the size of the other. And he could have sworn that the man had a single, large breast hanging from the center of his chest.

Shelly cursed too, but the blood was so loud in Cal's ears that he couldn't hear exactly what she said.

"George, why don't you bring our guests to their quarters?"

The man didn't hesitate, he simply rushed toward them. Shelly remained frozen, but Cal was suddenly imbued with courage. As the man lumbered toward them, his gait awkward, his right leg lagging behind, he guided Shelly behind him again and stepped forward.

When the man came within striking distance, Cal swung the crowbar with an upward trajectory. But when he was within a foot, he got his first real good look at the man, and all of his strength was suddenly sapped from him.

The man was stitched together like a jigsaw puzzle, pieces of rotting flesh sewn on his face, chest, and arms with thick, lace-like sutures.

It was Frankenstein's monster in the flesh.

The crowbar struck the thing that Justine had called George, but it bounced harmlessly off his hard stomach. Vibrations shot up Cal's forearms, and the crowbar fell from his hands.

The monster came to a stop and turned his stitched face to the ceiling and growled again.

Cal turned and ran.

Somewhere in the back of his mind, he knew that Shelly was running too, but his tunnel vision was so severe, his fear so palpable, that he couldn't even see where she had gone.

As he sprinted toward the door to the Seventh Ward that they had come through, he found Shelly already standing there, her palms bashing into the push bar over and over again.

"Open the door!" he screamed. "Open the fucking door, Shelly!"

She didn't turn; she simply continued to slam the bar with both hands.

"It. Won't. Open," she gasped.

Cal didn't stop running; at the last second, Shelly moved to one side and Cal rammed into the door hands first.

Pain shot up his wrists as his hands were crumpled backward.

He cried out as he immediately dropped to the floor.

"Fuck!" Shelly yelled. She started to remove her backpack, but a voice caused her to freeze.

"Don't kill them, George!" Justine's tone was desperate. "Don't kill them!"

Cal, still moaning from his smashed wrists, flipped onto his ass.

George was within a foot of him. As the massive beast leaned down until he was within inches of his face, Cal remained frozen in fear. The smell of rot and decay became so pungent that it made his eyes water, which thankfully obscured his view of the thick stitches, the mismatched skin tones that didn't line up right, and the horrible gash that ran from the corner of his mouth nearly to his ear.

The smell intensified when the beast named George spoke.

"Welcome to the Seventh Ward, Cal," the monster breathed.

Shelly said something to his left, but Cal was already spinning into a world of darkness.

Chapter 20

"WAKE UP, GEORGE."

Dr. Shaw leaned over the body, careful not to get too close in the event that the man on the gurney reacted as his brother had.

"George, it's time to wake up."

The man didn't stir, inciting a frown from Dr. Shaw.

What's going on? He should be waking now...he's been under so many times that he should have built up a tolerance by now. Unless...

"Nurse, how much nitrous did you give him?"

Justine turned to look at him, her face a lumpy, purple mess. He wasn't sure how she had managed to quiet George's twin, but it couldn't have been easy. Her nose was broken high on the bridge, she had a shiner under her left eye, and her lips, normally thin bordering on nonexistent, were swollen and split.

And yet the blood on her hands didn't appear to be her own.

Dr. Shaw should have been more specific; he should have told Justine to shut the man up without killing him, which was a distinct possibility given the complete and utter silence in the rest of the ward.

Still, he could deal with that later. His most pressing concern now was the man on the table before him.

The one he had named George after his late mentor.

"I gave him same as last time," Justine replied with a shrug.

A thin trail of blood trickled out of her right nostril, and she sniffed before wiping it away with the back of her hand.

Dr. Shaw turned back to his patient.

The man, like his brother, was completely nude, but unlike his brother, his leg wasn't the only thing that had been altered.

George was a mismatch of nearly a dozen individuals that he and Justine had lured into the Seventh Ward over the past few months.

His left ear belonged to a bus driver whose phone had died—thank God for shitty, irreplaceable phone batteries. Justine had managed to convince the man to come around side of the hospital under the pretext of using her cellphone.

George's right arm was from a vagrant that they had found sleeping outside the hospital. Enticing him inside had been even easier than the bus driver; all they'd had to do was leave the door ajar, and on a particularly cold night the man had come to them. They had tried to sew a prostitute's cheek to George's face, but that didn't work; no matter what they did, no matter what kind of glue or stitches they applied, it just wouldn't keep. Now George was left with a horrible scar that Dr. Shaw had done his best to suture. Problem was, every time the man opened his mouth, the wound reopened.

It didn't matter; after all, George wasn't winning a beauty contest anytime soon—that wasn't what his role was. Instead, they had opted to suture one of the prostitute's breasts to his chest. That part had been Justine's favorite, and he could have sworn that the woman had become aroused, her fat face flushing, her breath coming in shallow bursts.

And, of course, there was the most recent addition: his twin brother's leg. Dr. Shaw hoped that the fact that it was from his twin would help facilitate the healing process.

With each new addition, George started to change, and it wasn't only the increasingly pungent reek of rot. His personality became less cohesive, more reactive, bestial even.

There's someone inside me.

Dr. Shaw grabbed one of many damp cloths that had been used for the surgery and moved to the head of the gurney again. He pressed the cloth against the man's hot forehead and his eyes fluttered. A thin smile crossed his lips.

Without warning, George sputtered, then coughed. A brown sludge came flowing out of his mouth, and Dr. Shaw tilted the man's head to one side to make sure he didn't choke on it.

"Ah, I see that you are coming around," Dr. Shaw said. He couldn't help the massive grin that formed on his face. George may have been hideous, feverish, and weak, but he was alive. Which was progress, given what had happened with the others. Unlike the bus driver, vagrant, and prostitute, it had been an incredible risk luring George and his brother into the Seventh Ward. But the twins were exactly what Dr. Shaw was looking for: strong men, muscular men, men who could sustain and recover from multiple surgeries.

In the end, it had been worth it.

We're close.

George's eyes opened, and they shifted back and forth so quickly that Dr. Shaw feared that he was having a seizure. But after a few seconds they focused, and Dr. Shaw heard the exact same words that the man's brother had uttered more than an hour ago.

"What have you done to me?" George whispered.

Dr. Shaw ran a finger over the suture webbing on the man's cheek like a gentle caress. He could see the man's molars in the gash when he spoke, which was strange but at the same time very fascinating.

"Just trying to make you whole again, George. Just trying to make you whole."

George's face contorted in pain, and the several of the stitches that marked his shaved scalp and ran over his patchwork ear split. Blood slowly started to trickle from the wound.

"George? Who the—" He coughed again, bringing up more brown sludge. "—who the fuck is George? I've told you a hundred times, that's not my name."

Dr. Shaw shushed him.

"You need to relax…you need to heal so that I can show you to the world. So I can prove to them that I was right—prove to Dr. Mansfield that I was right all along."

As he stared down at the man on the gurney, he thought he saw tears begin to form in George's wide, brown eyes. Staring into those eyes, Dr. Shaw wondered what it would be like to transplant one of his brother's blue eyes.

"What did you do to me?" George whispered again, wetness spilling down his cheeks.

Dr. Shaw smiled.

Chapter 21

ROBERT BANGED AGAINST THE thick glass, but all this accomplished was to make his fist sore. He could see a *thing*—a lumbering giant of a man—rushing toward Cal and Shelly, and then he saw Cal hit him in the chest with his crowbar. The beast roared, and then his friends turned and ran. Robert pressed his face against the small window, trying desperately to keep his eye on them, to see what that *thing* was doing to them, but eventually they disappeared and he was left with only a view of Justine, standing there, that fucking smile plastered on her face.

"Hey!" he shouted. "Hey! Leave them alone!"

Robert yelled until his throat was raw, but it was no use; either Justine couldn't hear him, or she simply chose to ignore him. Crying now, Robert whipped around, splaying the flashlight around the room, looking for something—anything—that he might use to tear the thick metal door off its hinges.

There was nothing.

The gurney was covered in sheets soaked with what he assumed was long-dried blood, and there was a chair in the corner upon which he had thrown the cheap stuffed bunny on. The rest of the room was completely empty.

Robert collapsed on his knees, overcome with guilt and shame.

He was the reason why Shelly and Cal were here; he was the reason why they were about to be torn apart by that monster—or worse.

It might take them to the Marrow with it.

And he had a nagging feeling in the back of his mind that their experience wouldn't be the euphoria he had felt watching the gentle, rolling waves.

You have been chosen, Sean had said once.

Robert had no idea why, but he had a sneaking suspicion that was one of the reasons why he had gone and managed to come back. Maybe it was because he had spent so much time with Amy's quiddity. Or maybe it was something else entirely.

He didn't know.

He had no idea how or why he had come back from the one place that it was universally agreed upon that you could *never* return from.

He didn't know *anything*.

"Goddammit," he whispered, pounding his thighs with his fists. "Goddammit."

His flashlight flickered, and he instinctively shut it off, trying to save the dwindling battery power for when he might need it—*if* he needed it.

The irony of being locked in a cell for the mentally deranged as confusion washed over him was not lost on Robert.

And maybe he was insane. Maybe his wife and daughter dying had sent him on a spiral of insanity—his way of dealing with the loss. Maybe all of this—everything that had happened since—was simply a figment of his imagination.

But then he remembered Cal and Shelly. Real or not, he couldn't sit idly by while they were torn apart. He had to do something...anything.

Robert brought himself to his feet and slowly moved back to the doorway and peered out.

Justine was still there, but she was no longer staring ahead. Instead, she appeared distracted by something behind her.

It was Cal and Shelly.

They were walking side by side, their heads hung low, their feet shuffling.

What are they doing? Why are they coming back this way? Why didn't they run away?

His friends were moving toward what he suspected was a door on the other side of the hallway, one that was just out of his line of sight.

Tears were streaming down his cheeks now.

Why—?

But then Robert saw *it* again, and his breath caught in his throat.

It was indeed a man, or at least it had been at one point. Revulsion struck Robert like a punch to the solar plexus as he observed its patchwork skin, the breast in the center of its chest, the lopsided head and ear. It was as if it had been stitched together by some demented doctor.

Dr. Shaw is waiting for you.

Robert swallowed hard.

"Hey," he shouted, pounding on the glass again, this time with both fists. "Hey! Leave them—"

But a whisper from behind him cut him off.

"They can't hear you." The female voice was airy and hoarse, not unlike how Ruth Harlop's had been.

All of the blood drained from his face.

"This place…this place is meant to keep people in. Banging on the window won't help you."

Robert turned on his heels, while at the same time fiddling with the flashlight, trying to turn it on. The simple button, however, suddenly seemed to exceed his dexterity.

It was as if his hands were covered in thick mittens.

"No! No don't—please, Daddy, don't turn on the light."

Again, Robert froze. The voice was coming from the same location, but it was different—a child's voice.

The image of Amy, of the way she was in the photograph in his pocket, came to him then, and he swallowed hard.

It can't be.

But when the voice spoke again, it had changed once again into something else.

"I want you to fuck me!"

Robert pressed his back against the door, thoughts of his friends momentarily forgotten. He couldn't be sure if there was one woman in the room with him now, or three.

Robert finally managed to turn on the light. The beam was initially so bright that it momentarily blinded him, and he only heard someone—or *someones*—scrambling to get out of the way. When his eyes finally adjusted, he saw a crouched form by the corner of the room, opposite the chair. Relief washed over him when he realized that it was only one person, and not three, but the way she was crouched and huddled, her skin thin and leathery, her spinal cord jutting out, made him think of Ruth Harlop.

"Ruth?" he croaked.

There was no response.

He took a small step forward, but the elderly woman's back started to hitch, and he realized that she was sobbing.

He halted his forward advance.

This wasn't Ruth Harlop, a suspicion that was confirmed by her next sentence.

"Please," she whimpered, "don't let Daddy hurt me."

Robert shook his head, trying to think clearly.

Unlike with Justine, he was positive that this was an apparition, a quiddity—it had to be. There had been no one in the room with him moments ago.

But she had...what? A split personality?

Shelly's words in the car on the drive to Pinedale echoed in his mind.

Dr. Mansfield was kidnapped by someone with a split personality disorder.

His grip tightened on the heavy flashlight.

Could this be her? Could this old woman be the one that killed Dr. Mansfield?

"Who—who are you?" he managed at last.

The woman stopped sobbing and she slowly started to raise her head. Her eyes were dark, black pits, and her neck was split in an ear-to-ear gash.

Robert tried to force himself *through* the door behind him, to no avail.

She brought a finger to her lips.

"Shh, he's coming now. The doctor is in."

Robert's entire body stiffened.

"Wha—?"

But then a bang on the door jarred him out of his stupor, and despite the imminent danger that this woman posed, he spun around. His first thought was that it was going to be Justine, or worse, that *thing*, staring into the room, but it was neither.

Instead, he was greeted by the face of a young-looking man, probably in his mid to late twenties, with shaggy brown hair and dark circles ringing his eyes. His lips were pressed into a thin line.

Robert leapt backward.

"Dr. Shaw is here," he heard the old crone whisper as she faded away. "He's here...he's here...he's here..."

Chapter 22

"THAT'S IT," DR. SHAW clapped his hands together. "That's it! Put most of your weight on your...your *good* leg. Yes, yes, that's it! *That's it!*"

He couldn't believe his eyes. George managed to slide to the edge of the gurney, and by placing his arm over Nurse Justine's broad shoulders, he was partially standing. Shaw could see that the man's leg had shifted around the wound, the top half sliding a little from the bottom half—his brother's leg—but it appeared to be holding.

Dr. Shaw clapped again.

"Yes! This is..."

But he couldn't come up with an appropriate adjective to describe what he was seeing. Instead, he just reveled in watching his creation.

Justine grunted as she shouldered the brunt of the massive man's weight, her round face taking on an unnatural shade of crimson, but together they took their first step.

He's even tougher than I thought—than I could have ever hoped.

A waft of rot suddenly hit him, and Dr. Shaw grimaced. The smell was bad today, the worst ever, perhaps, but the leg wound appeared to be clear.

"Dr. Shaw? What next?" Justine asked in a strained voice.

Dr. Shaw mulled this over for a moment. The simple fact was that he had only half expected this to work...he had steeled himself for the distinct possibility that George would just topple, the transplanted leg tearing off, leaving him to bleed out. Even with Justine as a donor, the man had been through so much that the prospect of survival was next to nil. In his mind,

Dr. Shaw had gone so far as to picture having to put George in the freezer with the others, a long line of unsuspecting donors that had contributed their lives to this project.

But now that it had actually *worked*, he raced to figure out how he would finally prove his theory.

"I, uhh, I want to see if you can guide him around the gurney. Maybe—" He looked around, his gaze eventually falling on the wall about ten feet from where George and Justine presently stood. "Maybe take him for a walk to the wall. See if he can touch it, then come back."

Justine grunted an affirmative, and then they swiveled together. Dr. Shaw's eyes were locked on George's transplanted leg as they started to move. Again, the two halves seemed to slide out of sync, which was to be expected as the bone couldn't have fully healed so quickly.

But it held. It *fucking* held.

A smile crept onto the doctor's face.

The odd couple took another shuffling step forward, then another, George's transplanted leg sliding more than actively walking.

Eyes wide, Dr. Shaw watched as the duo made it to the wall. Both of them were breathing heavily from the effort, strained, exhausted, but they had actually made it.

Dr. Mansfield had claimed that it wasn't possible, that even if they managed to attach the body parts and the patient survived, there was no evidence to suggest that the person would acquire the split personalities of the donors.

Foolish, Dr. Mansfield had told him. *You have read too many science fiction books, Andrew. And this idea? The idea that multiple personality disorders are a result of two people trapped in one body?*

Well, that's foolish, too. It's a mental issue, a disability from frag-
mented minds. A disease that can be treated, if not cured. In your case,
however —

What about cell memory? Organ memory —

—unproven, pseudoscience bullshit, Andrew. Get your —

The image faded when Justine and George started to turn
and something happened.

At first, Dr. Shaw wasn't sure if the man's leg had given way,
or if Justine had simply crumpled under George's weight. Either way, they both went down in a heap, Justine and George
letting out hauntingly similar cries.

To Dr. Shaw's dismay, Justine was pulled on top of George,
and not vice versa. Her elbow struck a metal tray during her
fall, sending a kidney shaped plastic dish filled with surgical
tools into the air like metallic confetti.

"No!" Dr. Shaw shouted, hoping that the man's leg hadn't
been injured—or worse, torn off—in the fall. "No! Justine, get
off him!"

The nurse was startled, and paused before trying to roll onto
her back and stand.

She was too slow.

George, despite his obvious disabilities, was faster. The man
somehow managed to shift into a sitting position in one fluid
motion and his massive hand, the one that was his own, and
not the smaller, withered transplant, reached out and grabbed
nurse Justine's pale blue scrubs. She yelled and tried to scramble away on all fours, but George's grip was strong, and when
he yanked, she fell back into him. Justine's knee landed on
George's transplanted leg and Dr. Shaw heard a distinct tearing
sound.

"No!" he yelled. He was within a foot of the two of them
before the struggle promptly ended. During their scramble,

George had grabbed a scalpel, and he held it the soft white skin below Justine's chin.

"I'll kill her," George hissed. The sound whistled through the hole in the side of his face where the stitches had torn again.

Dr. Shaw surveyed the situation closely before acting. George's good arm was snaked around Justine's chest, holding her firm, while the one holding the knife had once belonged to the bus driver. It was gray and weak-looking compared to his other, but George's grip on the scalpel looked strong enough — at least strong enough to jab the blade into Justine's neck.

Dr. Mansfield's words suddenly echoed in his head.

Even if transplants work, there is no evidence that the patient would adopt the personalities of the donors. That's foolish.

Andrew felt the smile on his face start to grow.

Oh, really?

His eyes flicked to the expression of pure hatred on George's mangled, stitch-riddled face. The man and his brother had been high school guidance counselors, of all things, before Justine and he had lured them to the Seventh Ward.

Good, law-abiding individuals who'd had illustrious college football careers. Men that looked out for others, that tried to guide them to the right path in life.

The right profession, personal enlightenment.

Dr. Shaw started to beam.

"Yes," he said, his voice barely a whisper. "Yes, George, kill her...kill her...kill her..."

Chapter 23

ROBERT HEARD A MUTED beep from somewhere outside the door, and he instinctively took another step backward. He swung the flashlight around, making sure that the old, demented woman was gone, and after confirming that she indeed was, he moved even farther from the man with the shaggy hair.

His back bumped up against the gurney just as the door opened.

The man was shorter than Robert had thought, making it only to about his chin. And instead of some sort of weapon as he had partly expected, the doctor was holding a folder in his hands. Robert sized him up quickly, and then peered around him. To his dismay, he could no longer see Cal or Shelly, but the beast was gone as well.

He was torn over whether this was a good or bad thing.

Justine, however, was standing behind Dr. Shaw, the creepy smile still plastered on her pale face.

I can shove him—I can get by him and make a run for it.

Robert's eyes flashed to the keycard that hung on his hip.

But I won't get anywhere without one of those...

He realized then that the reason why Shelly and Cal had been forced back this way, why they hadn't sprinted back up to the first floor and left the way that they had come in, was that it was locked.

And they didn't have the key.

How fucking stupid are we to follow Justine in here? How absolutely retarded are we?

But at the time, they had been so surprised to actually see anyone in the abandoned hospital that their rational faculties had shut down.

Do you find yourself behaving strangely? Getting angry more than usual?

"Robert Watts?" the doctor asked, raising his gaze.

Robert noticed that the man had red streaks and dark bruises that nearly encircled his entire neck and throat.

"What the fuck do you want from me?" Robert spat. "Where are my friends?"

The doctor, sporting a white lab coat over scrubs that looked identical to Justine's, frowned and looked down at his file for a moment before snapping it closed.

"Robert Watts, my name is Dr. Andrew Shaw. I'm the psychiatrist-in-chief here in the Seventh Ward."

Robert blinked, his grip tightening on the flashlight.

"What? What the fuck are you talking about? The place has been closed for—"

"Tsk, tsk, Robert. I can assure you that this ward is, and has been, fully functioning for a good while now. Don't let"—he raised his eyes to the dark lights above—"the lack of power fool you. You know, the rising cost to keep the water running 'n' all that."

He snickered, and Justine joined in.

What the fuck?

Dr. Shaw stopped laughing.

"Please, Robert, sit up on the bed."

Robert looked behind him quickly, a grimace forming on his lips at the sight of the dark brown sheet that covered the bed.

"Robert?" He turned back to see Dr. Shaw staring at him with an eyebrow raised. "The gurney, please."

"No way," Robert replied bluntly. "I'm not getting up there. I want to see Cal and Shelly."

Dr. Shaw sighed.

"Your friends are fine, I assure you. I will see them after you...you are a—how can I say this—a *priority*. You have friends in high—" He laughed again. "—or low places, Mr. Watts."

What is he talking about? Is he talking about Sean? Does he know Sean?

When Robert still didn't move, Dr. Shaw's expression changed, his eyebrows lowering, his lips pulling downward at the corners.

"Get the fuck up on the gurney, Robert. Get up there or I'll call George," he hissed. "If you want to see your friends again, you better get the *fuck* onto that bed."

Robert quickly mulled his options, the vision of the freak with the stitches—*George*—flashing in his mind.

Fuck.

He backed up and slid his rear onto the end of the gurney, careful not to move too high and come in contact with the soiled top half of the sheet.

Is that the old woman's blood? Did she die in this room? Slit her own throat, maybe?

He leveled his gaze at Dr. Shaw, who cautiously approached, Nurse Justine in tow.

Or was it the good doctor? Justine, maybe? Is that why a clump of hair is missing from the back of her head? Because of a struggle with an old, demented woman?

"Good." Dr. Shaw turned to Justine. "Justine, bind his legs, please."

"Wha—what?" Robert stammered. But before he could fully comprehend what was going on, Justine had pushed by the doctor and was on him, both of her meaty hands pushing down on his right thigh.

The flashlight slipped from his hand and he seized.

After how careful he had been in the hall—making sure that Justine was just far enough away that if she felt so inclined to touch him, he would have been able to move away—it came down to this.

Predictable, expected, but wholly unavoidable.

Robert sucked in a breath and closed his eyes, expecting to be instantly transported to the Marrow. He was prepared to see the waves, the rolling waves crashing on the shore, and the fissure in the sky...the dark, foreboding sky filled with screams...

But none of this happened.

Robert's eyes flicked open, and he realized that Justine had already strapped his left ankle to the gurney.

"No," he moaned, but when she went to his other leg, he remained limp.

Confusion washed over him.

Why haven't I gone to the Marrow? What does this mean? Does it mean...does it mean that Justine is real?

Is any of this real?

"That's a good patient. I wish all of my patients were as obedient as you, Mr. Watts. It would make my life one hell of a lot easier."

Chapter 24

"I KNOW YOU'RE IN there, Dr. Mansfield. Kill this woman, kill her now. Then you will know, there's someone inside *you*."

George's eyes went wide, and the hand holding the knife started to tremble.

"I'm not Dr. Mansfield," he said, his voice, like his hand, shaking. "I don't know...I don't know who that is."

Dr. Shaw made a clucking sound with his tongue, and he crossed his arms in front of his chest.

"Of course you are. As you are Frank the bus driver, Julia the junkie whore, and Vincent the hobo. You're also your brother. And, last but not least, you are Dr. George Mansfield. You are all of these."

"What...what did you do to me? You turned me into some sort of freak. A rotting, disgusting *freak*!"

Dr. Shaw shook his head violently.

"No, no, no, not a freak. You are a medical experiment. Truth and witness to the fact that split personalities are not the result of something in the mind, but a transplant of organs. Do you think that it is a coincidence that you are using Dr. Mansfield's arm to hold the scalpel? Hmm?"

George chanced a glance down at the arm that held the blade, and his face drooped as if seeing it for the first time.

"What's happened to me?" he whispered, spit now dripping from his mouth and the hole in his cheek. "I think...I think I'm going insane...or maybe this is a dream and the only way to wake up is—"

Andrew's smile faded, as he anticipated what was going to happen next.

"No!" he roared and started toward the man, who still had Justine held tightly in his lap. The hand holding the scalpel moved away from Justine's throat, and it immediately went to his own. George released Justine, and, eyes wide, she scrambled to her feet.

"Out of the way!" Dr. Shaw screamed as she ran toward him. She was so thick that he had to step around her, and by then it was too late.

"This is just a dream," George whispered, and then he drove the scalpel deep into his neck just below the ear. His eyes bulged, and Andrew lunged at him. He grabbed the man's hand, trying desperately not to allow any further damage. Thankfully, it was George's weak hand, the transplanted one, and Andrew managed to pull it from the man's neck. Tossing the blade to the floor, he placed both hands over the wound, which had already sprayed his face and neck with hot blood.

He turned back to Justine.

"Get the gauze! Get the gauze and the sutures!" he shouted at her. For a second, her doughy face just stared at him. "Now! Get the—"

But a hand suddenly shot up and gripped his throat, and this time it wasn't George's weak hand.

It was his strong one.

Gasping, Andrew turned back to the man, staring into his stitch-filled face. His eyes were blazing, his hatred palpable.

In that moment, he was struck with two options: take his hands away from the man's wound and allow him to bleed out and tear at George's hand that was crushing his esophagus, or keep it as it was and fulfill his dream.

George would never kill. This had to be something else— *someone* else.

Vincent maybe? Or Julia? Julia got plain mean when she didn't have her fix.

As his vision started to narrow, a smile crept onto Dr. Andrew Shaw's face.

There's someone inside me.

Chapter 25

"HAVE YOU EVER HEARD thoughts that weren't your own? Have you ever thought that there was someone else inside your head?"

Robert grimaced through clenched teeth. His eyes were wide, locked on the blade that Dr. Shaw was bringing closer and closer to his bare calf. The tourniquet just below his knee had numbed the lower half of his leg, but the sheer sight of that gleaming scalpel made his heart race. He barely heard the words that the doctor was saying; he was locked up with both fear and trying to make sense of everything.

"You—you promised you would let my friends go," he managed to whisper. "Do what you want to me—but you have to let them go. They don't deserve to die here."

Dr. Shaw chuckled.

"Get the gauze ready, Justine." Then, to Robert, he said, "You see, that's the problem with people like you: you don't know what it means to actually let go—to really be free. To see the—"

A faraway look suddenly passed over Dr. Shaw's eyes and his scalpel hovered in midair. Robert instantly recognized the expression.

"—the Marrow?" he said softly, finishing the doctor's sentence for him.

The blissful look on Dr. Shaw's face became one of shock before transitioning into a grin.

"Oh, you're a knowledgeable one, aren't you? I was warned about you...the Goat warned about you."

Robert swallowed hard. The multiple mentions of the Goat were somehow making it more real. When James Harlop had first threatened that it was coming, he thought it was just the ramblings of a madman on the verge of dying a second time.

But now…

What the hell is the Goat?

For some reason, however, Robert just knew that it had something to do with the rift in the sky…the opening and the screams that echoed over the Marrow.

"What is the…the *Goat*?" he whispered.

Dr. Shaw shook his head and his expression hardened. Clearly, he too was frightened of the Goat.

"Hold him down, Justine."

The woman's hands tightened on his head, locking it in place. Although his arms and feet were bound, it was clear that they didn't want to risk him biting either of them. Justine's hands were cool and clammy on his skin, but they felt nothing like James Harlop's had.

She was alive, he was sure of it. As for Dr. Shaw, however…

"My friends," Robert whispered.

Dr. Shaw lowered the blade until it was only an inch from his calf.

"I asked you a question, Robert Watts."

Robert, teeth still clenched, his forehead soaked with sweat beneath Justine's hands, couldn't recall what exactly the man had asked. He kept glancing at the door, expecting Cal's face to fill the window, or Shelly's.

Pretty Shelly with the foul mouth who had saved him when he was sure that Patricia Harlop was going to lay her hands on him.

But there was no one there—no one was going to rescue him this time. There was only darkness.

If he wanted to get out of there alive, he was going to have to help himself.

"I asked if you have ever felt like there is someone else inside your head? Telling you what to think? What to say?"

Robert thought about this for a moment, about how he hadn't been acting like himself. He had been quick to anger, as Cal had pointed out. And the whole situation with Jacky…it was so unlike him.

But even when he had been under the grip of the Harlop Estate and the Harlop family, it had still been him performing those actions.

Dr. Shaw grew impatient and didn't wait for a response.

"Well I have, Robert. For as long as I can remember, there has been someone else in my head. And I can't get him out, because he is also" —with the hand not holding the scalpel, Dr. Shaw pulled down the front of his shirt, revealing the top of a thick, pink scar— "in here."

And with that, the doctor lowered the scalpel to the back of Robert's calf. He felt searing pain, but with the hands that tightened on his forehead, he couldn't see exactly what was happening.

But he felt it.

A scream bubbled in his throat and then echoed in the small room, threatening to deafen them all. Robert tried to squirm, tried anything to break free, but Justine's hands and the leather straps were too strong.

Hot liquid soaked his leg, and he knew that the man was in the process of removing his calf.

"Please!" he cried through teared vision. "Please, dear God, let me out of here!"

Dr. Shaw didn't reply; he remained focused on his task.

Robert squeezed his eyes together tightly, biting the inside of his lip so hard that he tasted blood. Darkness threatened to wash over him, but he forced it away.

Shelly and Cal were here somewhere, and he had to save them.

He had to find a way out.

Robert forced himself to hyperventilate, trying everything to stay conscious as Dr. Shaw performed whatever hellish surgery he was doing down there.

Time passed, time that stretched out, much as it had been in the Harlop Estate. A disoriented Robert had no idea if an hour or ten minutes had passed.

Eventually, however, he felt a pressure release from the back of his leg, as if a heavy load had been removed. This was quickly followed by an incredible tightness that stretched all the way across his shin.

He's sewing me up now. It's almost time.

Shelly's pretty face, her too-red lips in a pout, moving in for a kiss, flashed in his mind.

This can't be it. I won't let it.

A hackneyed plan began to form in his mind. One that was as dangerous as it was foolish.

And insane; it was probably a little insane.

But with the leather straps and Justine's thick hands on his head, he could think of no way to get out of here...at least not in the physical world.

More time passed, and eventually Justine let go of his head and started to fiddle with a syringe.

"I'm sorry about the pain, Robert. Truly, I am. But there just aren't many drugs left, and sometimes..." He let his sentence trail off.

Robert's eyelids started to flutter, and as expected, Dr. Shaw came right up next to him. He was holding something in his hand, something that looked like a pork shoulder, straight from the butcher. Only it was smaller, and was very familiar.

Robert turned his head away from the gruesome sight.

"Robert," Dr. Shaw said, moving even closer. "I need you to see this. You should be proud; you are going to be part of something—"

Robert waited until the man was so close that he could smell his sweat emanating from beneath his lab coat. And then he quickly turned back, his eyes flipping forward.

Although his wrists were bound, his hands were still fairly mobile. Robert stretched his fingers as far as the strap would allow, and then he clamped his hand down on Dr. Shaw's wrist.

The man's eyes immediately went wide, then started to turn black. He tried to pull away, but Robert's grip was like iron.

"Justine! Justine!" the doctor shouted, but it was too late. His gaze lowered to Robert. "Wha—what have you done?"

Robert's grip held fast, and as he stared into the man's black eyes, he started to see little specks of white.

Tiny, rolling whitecaps.

I'm going back...

PART III – A Picture of Amy

Chapter 26

"**WHAT DO YOU THINK** they're doing to him?" Cal asked softly. There was an extended pause, and for a second, he thought that maybe Shelly had fallen asleep. His outstretched hand reached for her in the dark. It grazed her hair, and he instinctively pulled it back.

"That you?" she asked.

"Yeah, just checking to see that you were still awake. I asked if you knew what they were doing to him?"

Shelly sighed, a pained expression.

"Fuck if I know."

Cal felt tears coming on, but he forced them away.

That *thing*—that abomination—had taken them to their own cell and ordered them inside. They had had no choice but to relinquish their flashlights, as it was all they could do to avoid being touched by the rotting creature that Justine called George, of all things.

The name, however unfitting, did have a strangely familiar ring to it.

Then the monster had promptly left them alone in the dark. To wait for…Cal couldn't even imagine for what.

"You have your cellphone?"

"No. I think I—I think I dropped it."

Cal bit his lip and waited. He had a sneaking suspicion that Shelly had given up, that she was going to just roll over and die. It was in the way her responses were short, abbreviated, immediately followed by heavy exhalations.

It reminded him, strangely, of when his friend Mike had died.

In that moment, Cal wanted nothing more than to have some light source to be able to look into her eyes. To see what was in there...*deep* inside there.

He swallowed hard, and pushed the morbid thoughts away.

Shelly was his friend, and getting that feeling back from all those years ago wasn't worth the price she would have to pay...was it?

"Do you remember the doctor's name? That one that was, uhh, killed?"

"Mansfield or some shit."

"His first name? Was it George?"

There was another pause, and Cal waited patiently. Aside from their breathing, the rest of the room was thankfully silent. If they heard nothing for a few more minutes, Cal had convinced himself that he would search around in the darkness with his hands, trying to find some way out. Or something to use to *get* them out.

Even with things like George lurking about in the Seventh Ward.

"Yeah," Shelly said at last. "I think it was...you don't think—wait, you think that that *thing* is—"

"I don't know," Cal admitted with a shrug. "But you saw its face...it was—fuck, I dunno, it was multiple people all stitched together."

Just thinking about the sight of the horrible sutures criss-crossing the man's cheeks and mouth was enough to bring about an involuntary shudder.

"Maybe...but what does it matter, Cal? We're stuck here, while they are torturing Robert. All while we just sit here in the dark waiting to die...to be taken to the Marrow. To rot for eternity."

"Die? I'm not going to die, Shelly. I'm going to send this abomination to—"

"I told you guys to take this seriously, I *fucking* told you guys," Shelly interjected.

Cal reached out with the intention of hugging her, but he missed and ended up striking her in the shoulder. To his surprise, she actually leaned into him. She smelled of sweat, but Cal didn't mind. He hugged her tight for a moment, relishing human contact. Her back hitched slightly, but then she seemed to stiffen and pulled away from him.

"You're right, Cal. I'm not giving up. Fuck that."

Cal smiled in the darkness.

"Let's go find Robert, then," he said.

"Fuck, I completely forgot," Shelly said excitedly. Her change in attitude was so sudden that Cal felt his face flush with warmth.

Was it hugging me that did that? Was that it?

"What? What is it?"

He heard some rummaging, then a zipper being opened, but Shelly still didn't answer.

"What?" he asked again, his heart rate picking up.

Then he heard something else—a strange clicking sound that he didn't recognize.

"Shelly, what are you—?"

But his words were cut short as the cell was suddenly awash in bright light. Cal instinctively brought a forearm up to shield his face and cowered from the blaze.

Blinking rapidly, his eyes slowly adjusted enough to make out Shelly's smiling face.

"I forgot all about the blowtorch," she said, her smile growing. "Let's blast our—"

"Wait," Cal interrupted, "they took our flashlight and crowbar, but didn't take your backpack?"

"Fucking geniuses they aren't," Shelly replied, still smiling. "Probably didn't even—"

But a small voice from behind them wiped the expression away instantly.

"Have you seen it?" the voice asked.

Shelly whipped the blowtorch around so quickly that it made trails across Cal's vision.

Although the blowtorch was incredibly bright, it didn't spread well, and while they could make out an old-fashioned wooden bed covered in a sheet a few feet from them, they couldn't see who had spoken.

Then the voice spoke again, and Cal froze.

"Have you seen my ear?"

Shelly moved the blowtorch toward the man's voice again, leaning forward hesitantly. A man stepped from the shadows, and a scream caught in Cal's throat.

Chapter 27

WAVES...GENTLY CRASHING SURF...

Robert Watts's eyes slowly opened, and he found himself back at the place he had so desperately wanted to return to.

He was on the shores of the Marrow—only this time, he wasn't just an observer, as he had been when he had been grabbed by James Harlop in the basement of the Harlop Estate. Now, after wrapping his fingers around Dr. Andrew Shaw's arm, he was actually *here*.

Robert was standing with his feet slowly sinking into the warm, soft sand. He looked down at his toes, and then slowly raised them all at once, reveling at how amazing the sand felt as it spilled between and over the top of his foot. It felt like miniature balls of velvet cascading over his skin.

A sigh escaped his mouth, a sound that seemed to have a viscosity to it, spilling from the open orifice and moving slowly through the air. He raised his gaze and watched as the sound moved away from him, but it eventually faded, leaving him staring at the amazing surf. The waves, gentle yet powerful, lapped at the milk-and-coffee-colored shore but six feet from where he stood.

He should have been afraid; based on everything that he had read, everything that Shelly had told him, he should have been very afraid, terrified even, at the prospect of never returning home. But he only felt one pervasive emotion: pure, unadulterated fulfillment. It was as if someone had painlessly guided a catheter into his heart and had filled it with love.

The waves were hypnotizing, and he stared at them as they broke on the shoreline, all seemingly identical. He watched to see if they changed, some subtle difference based on unseen air or water currents, or movement of fish or vegetation that were hidden just out of sight below the crystal blue waters. It was impossible, he knew; the waves *had* to be different. But no matter how long he watched—which could have ranged anywhere from a few seconds to hours—they were all identical, breaking at the exact same time, frothing the exact same distance on the velvety sand.

For some reason, Robert felt compelled to move, and he lifted his right foot from the sand, almost giddy at the sensation of the tiny granules clinging to his bare skin. After the surface tension had broken, his feet seemed to slide, and in seconds he found himself at the shore. He squatted and extended his hands, intent on cupping the Marrow Sea in his hands, seeing if he could break the hypnotic symmetry of it all, but before they touched the water, a voice called out to him and he froze.

It was a voice he hadn't heard in a few months, but it was one he knew well.

It was the voice of his late nine-year-old daughter, Amy.

"Daddy? Is that you, Daddy? It's dark in here, Daddy." Her voice was strained and so utterly out of place in this holy sea of serenity. Robert retracted his hands and his heart began to race. "Daddy? You promised me that it would be beautiful here, that it would be—"

"Amy!" he croaked, unable to control himself. His eyes desperately scanned the surf, trying to find Amy out there somewhere. But he saw nothing different from a few moments ago. Tears began to spill down his cheeks. "Amy?" he asked again, his voice more desperate now.

"Daddy, please—"

Then something happened—something that had happened before.

Something was not right in the Marrow.

The sky, full of soft, fluffy clouds and gentle, warming sunlight, suddenly flickered. And then lightning split the atmosphere, its appearance startling during what he considered the perfect summer day. It was as if the place were powered by cheap incandescent lighting, flickering on and off, becoming less luminous with each flicker.

"Amy!" he cried out, rising to his feet.

But before he could even finish the word, the sun suddenly blinked out. In its place, the clouds became roiling flames, a strange bubbling cauldron of fire just above his head. Gasping for air now, Robert tried to step backward, but he found himself unable—his feet seemed to be stuck. His eyes darted downward, and he screamed.

The sand, moments ago so soft and inviting, had become a thick, black tar, gripping his feet and ankles. It even seemed to be moving—not just bubbling and boiling over, but he thought he could see *hands* down in the mud. Gnarled, horrible things that formed and then burst, some of them making fists, others reaching for him, popping and collapsing only inches before making contact.

"What the fuck!" he yelled, trying to yank his feet free. With an incredible pull, his right foot came loose, and he took a large step, but before he even put it down again, a hand formed, reached up, and grabbed his heel, tugging it back to the muddy ground.

"No!"

Lightning lit up the sky, an incredible blast, drawing his gaze upward. The flames were still there, but now he could see distinct outlines in them.

Faces…it's filled with faces.

As he watched in sheer horror, the faces grew in size, their flaming outlines masking his own expression: mouths wide, nostrils flaring, eyes bulging. They rolled in and out of focus, bubbling to the surface before receding again. Robert, not believing what he was seeing, blinked rapidly, trying to clear his vision. But each time he opened his eyes again, he could have sworn there were more and more faces popping in and out of existence, a nose of this person becoming the eye of another, the mouth of one becoming the ear of someone else.

Until he could see millions of these tortured expressions stretching over the infinite expanse of the sea.

"Welcome, Robert," a low, gravelly voice behind him suddenly said. "I've been expecting you."

Sweat pouring off his entire body, Robert turned hard, yanking his feet from the mud. The hands that held him rooted unexpectedly released, and he over spun, spiraling onto his hands and knees.

Robert slowly raised his gaze, his breathing coming in short bursts.

There was a man in a faded jean jacket only a dozen feet from him. He was sporting a wide-brimmed black hat pulled low, which cast a shadow over his face, and was sitting atop a boulder—one that he immediately recognized.

He didn't need to see the letters etched in the rock to know that it was Patricia Beatrice Harlop's tombstone.

"Who—who are you?" Robert whispered.

Chapter 28

"DON'T COME ANY CLOSER," Shelly warned, waving the blowtorch at arm's length. Cal cowered behind her, peering over her left shoulder, eyes wide. "You come *any* closer and I'll light you up, I swear it."

It was difficult to gauge the man's reaction, partly because he seemed confused, but mostly because he was missing the left half of his face.

"I'm—I'm—" the man began, starting toward them again.

Shelly extended the blowtorch even farther.

"Stop!" she shouted, and the man's forward advance immediately ceased. For nearly a full minute, none of them moved. In fact, it was difficult to tell if any of them even breathed; the only sound in the room was the hissing of the blowtorch.

Cal used the momentary reprieve to observe his surroundings.

The room was small, square, the walls covered in peeling beige paint. There was the bed in the center, and what might have once been a window at the back now covered in a thick piece of plywood. And then there was the man. He was young, mid-thirties, maybe, dressed in a gray track suit. He had short brown hair and a neatly cropped beard. But his face was horrifying, rivaling even the abomination that was George. The left side had been completely removed, revealing a disgusting, glistening network of fibrous tissue. The eye on that side was missing, in its place a black pit within which it used to be housed.

Cal felt a bout of nausea hit him then, but he fought the urge to vomit, knowing that if the thin veneer of calm that encased this quiddity broke, the blowtorch in Shelly's hand, no matter how menacing with its blue-white flame, wouldn't save them.

As it was, he swallowed hard, a simple act that seemed to reanimate the man. The side of his face that still had skin, the side that was still *human*, dropped.

Cal thought that maybe he was frowning, or grimacing, but it was impossible to tell for certain.

"I'm sorry," he said softly, lowering his good eye.

Cal felt Shelly tense before him, and thought that maybe she was losing her nerve. He squeezed her sides gently, silently encouraging her.

"Who—who are you?" she stuttered.

The eye raised again and leveled itself at Shelly and Cal.

"My name is Danny Dekeyser," he replied simply.

"What are you doing here?"

The man shrugged and looked like he was going to step forward again, but Shelly shoved the torch and he stopped.

"I was cleaning...I was cleaning and then..." His voice trailed off. His hand slowly made its way to his face, gently probing the missing skin, the empty socket. "Then *it* got me."

Cal shuddered.

He needed no explanation as to what *it* was.

George.

The blowtorch suddenly flickered, and he heard Shelly gasp. She reached up and fiddled with the gas knob, and it thankfully roared back to life before blinking out.

Time was running out, Cal knew. He wasn't sure how much gas or propane or whatever the fuck the torch ran on was left, but he couldn't imagine much.

And they still had to use it to take out the hinges on the door, to get out of here, to grab Robert, and get the fuck as far away from the Pinedale Hospital—the Seventh Ward—as his chubby legs would carry him.

He decided to take things into his own hands.

"What do you want?" he asked, trying, but failing, to sound assertive.

This seemed to confuse Danny for a moment, and he just stood there, his lower lip quivering.

"I just want to go home," he said at last, and Cal felt a sudden pang of sadness for the young man. He was instantly reminded of Patricia Harlop who had been so thin that, like this man, her cheekbones seemed to be devoid of skin. And how confused she had been, trapped on this side when she so obviously belonged on the other.

That she belonged in the Marrow.

Cal wasn't sure what to say next. Evidently, Shelly didn't either, as she remained silent as well.

After a moment, Danny repeated the phrase, only this time his voice had a desperate quality to it that hadn't been there before.

"Home...I just want to go home."

Shelly cleared her throat.

"We can help you," she whispered. "We can help you, but first we need to get out of this room—out of the Seventh Ward."

Just the mention of the 'Seventh Ward' seemed to make the man recoil.

Cal recalled the horrific sight and smell of the creature that Justine had called George, and now it was his turn to shudder.

"You—you can help me go home?" he asked, his voice so low that Cal had to strain to hear him over the sound of the blowtorch.

Shelly nodded.

"Yes, we can help you, but we have to get out of here first."

The man looked up again.

"You can help all of us?"

A chill shot up and down Cal's spine.

All?

As if on cue, the shadows on either side of Danny Dekeyser started to shimmer and move. A second later, others began to step forward, all of them with downcast eyes.

This time, Cal managed to stifle his scream, but his hands that gripped Shelly's sides squeezed so tightly that she gasped.

Chapter 29

"I'M SURPRISED YOU DON'T recognize me, Robert Watts," the man in the black hat said, a hint of sarcasm on his tongue.

Robert just stared.

The man reached up slowly, and for a moment Robert thought that he was going to pull the hat back, to reveal his face, and a sudden revulsion over came him. Then the man chuckled, a horrible, grating sound that only made his nausea worse.

Robert's guts roiled.

Instead of lifting it, the man pulled the hat even lower, the shadow that had previously shown his chin now covering the top buttons of his jean jacket as well.

"I've been called many things over the years, Robert. I go by Leland now—Leland Black—but some people still insist on calling me the Goat."

The man waited and Robert felt a chill course through him.

The Goat is coming…

And then he remembered his discussion with the online entity known as LBlack.

His heart skipped a beat.

How could I have not realized the connection earlier? Has this…man…been stalking me? How? Why?

These and more questions ping-ponged about Robert's brain.

"What do you want from me?" he croaked, still trying, and failing, to come to terms with all of this.

Again, the man chuckled.

"You came to me, remember? What do *you* want?"

Robert mulled this over for a second.

Answers…I want answers.

"My daughter—Amy—I heard her voice…"

"Ah yes, nine-year-old? Blonde hair? About yea big?"

Robert swallowed hard.

"If you hurt her—"

Leland laughed again.

"She's not here, Robert—not now, anyway. And besides, I would never hurt family. But there is someone else here...someone who's not happy that you took him from the other world."

The man waited expectantly, and then an image of James Harlop appeared in Robert's mind. He shook his head, trying to clear the suddenly vivid picture of the man, complete with the gaping, ragged hole beneath his chin.

Another voice suddenly broke the ubiquitous screams and groans above.

"I'm not done with you yet!" the voice yelled—James's voice.

"So, Robert," Leland continued, "I think it's in your best interests to tell me why you are here..."

As before, an image suddenly came to mind. The image of Sean Sommers, complete with his black suit and navy peacoat.

If Robert could've seen the man in the jean jacket's face then, he wouldn't have been surprised if he were grinning.

"Ah, I should have known...should have known that this was Sean's meddling."

Robert's expression became a mask of confusion. He was certain that he hadn't said anything out loud.

Time slowed as the man's shoulders seemed to slump on his wiry frame.

"Question is, what does *Sean* want with you? It can't just be to send psychopaths like James Harlop here, can it? I'll give him this much, it was brave to send *you* of all people to this place."

Robert pulled himself to his feet, wiping the mud from his hands on his bare thighs.

"We can ask him together, maybe."

"He's...he's here?"

Leland laughed.

"No, not now. But he will be. Eventually everyone crosses through the Marrow, Robert." The man paused, then continued, his voice more serious now. "What do you know about Sean, Robert? Hmm? You look at me with such disgust, disdain, leaving me to wonder if you look at him the same way? Hmm? What do you *really* know about him?"

The answer was obvious.

He knew nothing about Sean Sommers.

"Well, then. We wait. After all, I have all the time in the world. You, on the other hand..."

Robert suddenly felt a sharp pain in the back of his left leg, and he looked down.

"Oh god," he muttered.

His left calf was almost completely gone, and blood flowed from the wound, soaking the back of his leg. Where it dripped to the ground, the muddy surface seemed to froth excitedly. The shock of the blood sent him reeling, and he fell on his ass.

What is this place?

Robert looked up again, and was so surprised that Leland was standing above him now. He tried to scramble away, but the muddy hands were back, holding him in place.

Leland slowly bent, his hat still tucked low. And then he reached out, and Robert did his best to recoil.

It was no use; he seemed rooted in place, every single one of his muscles seizing as if gripped by tetanus.

The man's hand stretched and then it gripped his wounded calf.

Pain erupted throughout his entire body, and suddenly it wasn't just the sky above that was engulfed in flames, but he was as well.

"We're just going to wait, Robert. Wait for—"

But then something happened.

The sky lit up with lightning again, and Leland's head snapped upward, revealing, for the first time, his face.

Robert screamed. Even as Leland Black's outline started to shimmer and fade, the sky above brightening, the fire dying down, he screamed.

"No! No! *No!*" Leland roared.

Robert Watts kept on screaming, even as his body was slowly returned to the land of the living.

Chapter 30

CAL COUNTED SIX QUIDDITY, but the way that they moved in and out of the shadows, there could have easily been twice that number.

There was Danny, another young man about his age missing part of his chest, a thin woman wearing a shirt so tight that he could make out every curve of her ample, single breast and the track marks that peppered the inside of her arms like dozens of bee stings. There was also the old, naked woman, the one who would occasionally break out into laughter. There was also a short black man missing an arm, and a mountain of a man, one that looked like George, but at the same time didn't; he was more *whole*. Still, he had to prop himself up because of a missing leg.

Every last one of them a tortured soul caught between worlds.

"We will...we'll help all of you get home," Cal said hesitantly.

Danny turned to those around him. There was a silent exchange of sorts, and Cal got the sneaking suspicion that their fate rested in whatever was said...or was not said.

"Well?" Shelly asked impatiently. "We have a deal or not? You guys stay there, let me take this door down, then we'll come back for you."

Danny nodded.

"We just...we just want—"

"—yeah, we get it. You just want to go home. Fuck, don't we all."

Cal grimaced at Shelly's bluntness. Still, what did it matter now? If these quiddity wanted to attack them, attach themselves to them, touch them, diddle them, do whatever the fuck they wanted, a handheld blowtorch wasn't going to save them.

"Good," Shelly said suddenly. "Now I'm going to turn around and get to work on this door, and Cal here is going to keep his eye on you guys. Any of you move toward the door, and…"

Again, Cal was incredulous.

"Umm, Shelly, I don't even—" *have a flashlight,* he was going to say, before Shelly drove her elbow into his side. He grunted, and was for once thankful for the spare tire that pretty much coated his entire body.

Then she turned around quickly, spinning with reckless abandon. Cal had to lean backward in order to avoid getting burnt from the torch.

Shelly set to work with the confidence of an expert mechanic, putting the hot flame up against the upper hinge of the thick metal door.

At first Cal just stared at the darkness behind them, the one that he knew held the quiddity of at least six people. But this was incredibly unnerving, and he felt himself beginning to crack. Even though it was nearly completely black in the room, he convinced himself that he could see some shadows moving, pulsing forward and backward.

What was he supposed to do? Even if they were suddenly on him, if he could actually *see* them, what was he going to do about it?

Shelly had been right; they knew nothing of these people— they had no book or gas mask or fireplace poker to bind them to.

They were truly helpless.

Instead of driving himself mad with things outside of his control, he turned to Shelly. She had made quick work of the first hinge, and was now on to the second. Despite their sturdy appearance, apparently the Seventh Ward architects hadn't considered psychiatric patients with flaming tools.

The light was so bright, in such contrast to the space behind them, that Cal had to look away as the flame licked the metal hinge. He was in awe of the fact that Shelly was even capable of being as close as she was, seeing as the sparks sprayed at least a foot from the point of contact.

There was a lot he didn't know about his sexy ghostbusting compadre, it seemed.

She pulled the flame away from the door for a moment.

"Cal, put both hands on the door," she instructed, and Cal immediately obeyed.

The door was cold to the touch, and he became distinctly aware that he was presenting himself to the quiddity behind him. He felt like he was being admitted to a supernatural prison.

"Now what?"

Shelly suddenly shut off the blowtorch and after the tracing in his eyes faded, they were once again immersed in darkness.

"Let go," she whispered.

"Let go?"

"Let go," Shelly repeated.

"Fuck—let go, then what?"

"Then we fucking run, Cal. Run as fast as you fucking can."

Chapter 31

ROBERT'S EYES SNAPPED OPEN, and they veritably bulged from his head, a scream caught in his throat. He could still smell his own burning flesh where Leland had gripped him.

What happened? How did I come back?

He glanced around quickly, and realized that Justine and Dr. Shaw had since left the room, leaving him in near darkness. He stretched his neck, trying to move to a sitting position, but then his head fell back down again.

The straps on his wrists and ankles were still tightly bound.

Robert shut his eyes and tried to make sense of what had happened, but all he saw were the faces in the fiery sky, faces that eventually morphed into one that he recognized: Amy's.

Help me, Daddy, you promised...

Tears ran down his cheeks, and he started to sob.

How did I get from moving into a new home with Wendy and Amy to here? To being tied up on a gurney in the Seventh Ward of an abandoned hospital, shuttling back and forth between the living and the dead?

But he knew; he knew how he had gotten here.

It was Sean Sommers's doing.

Leland's words suddenly echoed in his head: *How much do you really know about him? About Sean?*

Robert heard a scratching sound, and his eyes immediately snapped open.

There was someone directly beside him fiddling with the leather strap on his right wrist.

"What the fuck?" Robert whispered, trying again to move away.

The man looked up at him with sad, rueful eyes. He was about Robert's height, maybe a little taller, with a medium build. His face was angular, and he had glasses resting on the chest of his white lab coat.

"What are you doing to me?" Robert whispered.

"I'm sorry, but you were shaking and I...and I..." He let the sentence trail off.

"You what? Are you working with Dr. Shaw?" He lowered his voice and glared at the man. "Have you come for more of my...my *body*?"

There was a pause as the man seemed to mull this over. Then he lifted his glasses and put them on the bridge of his nose. He looked older now, mid-fifties, maybe.

"You were going into shock—a seizure—so I did the only thing that I could. I touched you."

Robert opened his mouth to say something, but then he hesitated. He squinted at the doctor, thinking hard.

"Are you...are you Dr. George Mansfield?"

The doctor sighed.

"Yes."

And then realization swept over him. The doctor—the one that had been dismembered but who was now mysteriously whole—had touched his body here, in the real world, and it was his touch that must have brought him back from the Marrow.

Robert swallowed hard, and he felt guilty at the vehemence of his previous comments. This man had helped him.

Saved him.

What it meant for Dr. Mansfield, however, was unclear, but Robert thought that the man's actions wouldn't be without penalty.

"Thank you," he whispered. The man grunted an affirmation, then the clasp on his wrist jangled and the wrap came free.

Robert immediately pulled his arm away from the man, careful not to touch him, and then he set to work on the other strap.

When both straps were released, he alternated rubbing his wrists. There were thick red binding marks on each and a dull ache in his bones. Dr. Mansfield hadn't been lying when he'd said he was seizing; his body must have been thrashing pretty hard to generate such a deep soreness.

With his upper body now free, he sat up, crying out at the pain that shot up his right calf.

After several deep breaths through clenched teeth, Robert finally collected himself.

"Why?" he asked Dr. Mansfield, who had respectfully taken a step back from the gurney.

The man shrugged.

"I swore an oath—an oath to save lives, Robert." The man looked down at his hands, and the corners of his lips turned downward. "It doesn't matter what form I take."

Robert eyed the man quizzically. Unlike the members of the Harlop family, Dr. Mansfield seemed to be acutely aware of his situation.

Of the fact that he was, indeed, dead.

A loud crash from somewhere outside his room suddenly drew his gaze from the doctor to the window to the hallway. There was a dim glow of light coming from somewhere just out of view, and Robert suddenly snapped back to reality.

Cal and Shelly were here somewhere.

"I have to get out of here," he muttered.

He quickly reached down and began undoing the strap on his left ankle. Then he moved to his right, but his eyes locked on his calf and he froze.

There was a massive chunk of skin and muscle missing, but this wasn't the most unnerving thing. There were three dark, burnt smudges that extended almost all the way around his now much thinner lower leg. And they ended in sharp points.

Leland's handprint... where he touched me.

Robert tried to remember that man's face that he had caught a glimpse of when the man had turned his gaze upward, but he couldn't. His mind had erected a mental block, protecting him from the horror. Just thinking about it, however, made his entire being well with anxiety and disgust.

Robert shook these feelings away and finished unstrapping himself. With a wince, he managed to lower himself off the gurney. Pain shot up his entire right leg, but he was at least thankful that Leland had cauterized the wound, stopping the bleeding.

That was something, at least.

With a limp, he managed to shuffle forward. He found his clothes balled on the floor and quickly put them on, his hand immediately going to the front right pocket. His fingers began massaging Amy's photograph.

Then he looked around. When his eyes fell on the red LED light by the door, his heart sunk.

"I think I can help with that," Dr. Mansfield said suddenly, and Robert turned to him inquisitively. The man was holding a keycard up to the limited light, and Robert couldn't help but smile.

He held it out to him, and Robert carefully took it, making sure not to make contact. Then he went to the door and pressed it up against the reader. It beeped, then turned green.

"Alright, let's go find Cal and Shelly...and Dr. Shaw," he said to himself, before pulling the door wide and stepping into the hallway.

Chapter 32

The sound of the door falling inward was impossibly loud. Cal cringed, but immediately jumped over it and into the hallway, thankful to be out of the room full of ghosts, even if they were the good guys.

Yeah, good ghosts...what the hell is the world coming to?

Shelly quickly followed him out, and then he couldn't help but turn back to the room that they had just escaped from. With the door gone, some ambient lighting—*where is the light coming from? Is there a window somewhere? Aren't we belowground?*—and with a heavy squint, he focused on Danny's outline. The man took a small step forward, and other figures at his sides, the other quiddity, stepped forward as well. For an instant, Cal thought that they were going to continue moving, to renege on their agreement and come crashing into the hallway with them. But they stopped, and Cal thought he saw Danny's lips move, mouthing the word, *Home*.

Cal nodded, then turned to Shelly when the quiddity receded back into the shadows from whence they came.

She had a wide look in her eyes, and her blonde hair was clinging in sweaty strips to her forehead. It was then that he realized her bravado, her courage, had been sapped, that what had happened in the room had taken it from her.

It was up to him now.

But home...

As if reading his thoughts, Shelly said, "Home? How can we send them all home?"

Cal reached for her, pulling her in close.

"Shh," he said, his eyes darting back to the now dark room.

Shelly pushed him away and put the blowtorch back in her backpack and zipped it, after first checking that the end had cooled enough to not risk melting the bag. After she was done, she looked up at him again, but this time when she spoke, her voice was softer.

"How, Cal?"

Cal bit his lip as he thought about it.

Yeah, Cal? How can we find an object that means something to six or seven tortured souls? Souls that we haven't met before? We don't even now their names...

"We'll—I'll think of something. But for now, let's find Robert. Maybe he knows what to do."

Shelly slipped the bag over her shoulder and stood.

"And Frankenstein? What about him and his fucking monster? I haven't heard—"

A bellow suddenly ripped through the hallway, echoing up and down for so long that Cal thought that it would continue on forever. Eventually, however, the sound faded, and he was left in the near darkness again, staring at Shelly with identical, horrified expressions.

Yeah, there was also *that* to deal with.

He hoped to Christ that Robert had some ideas.

The sound of a beep and a door opening behind him made him spin on his heels. Shelly instinctively moved behind him, but without his crowbar, Cal felt like an incredibly inept ninja in a black bathrobe. So he did what any man would do in his situation: he primed his body to run.

And he almost did—he almost ran. But when the door opened and a haggard-looking Robert stepped out, he froze instead. Unsure of what he was seeing, if it was real or not, he simply gaped.

Shelly, on the other hand, gasped.

"Robert!" she exclaimed, and then ran to him, nearly knocking Cal down in the process. But when she made it to within ten feet of him, she stopped cold.

Cal suddenly regained control of his body and also stepped forward.

"Shelly? What's wrong?" When she didn't answer, he picked up his pace. "Robbo? You okay?"

The man had a far-off look in his eyes, one that Cal recognized after his encounter with James Harlop in the basement.

Did he…?

"I'm fine," he said suddenly. Cal's long-time friend took a step forward, but it was labored with his right leg not so much bending as it was dragging. And he was grimacing.

Shelly pointed at him, and Cal thought that the woman had finally snapped. He reached out to lower her arm, but she resisted.

And then he saw it too.

There was a man behind Robert, slowly creeping forward. He was wearing a lab coat and had an old-fashioned pair of glasses on his nose, the kind with the beaded strings that librarians had rendered clichéd.

"Uhh, Robert," he said slowly. "You might want to come over here."

Robert limped forward another two feet.

"Hurry, Robbo…there's someone behind you!"

Chapter 33

"THIS IS DR. MANSFIELD," Robert said calmly, making room for the doctor to step forward. Cal's jaw drooped, and he thought he saw Shelly visibly gulp.

"Wha—wha—what?" Shelly blubbered.

"I'm—I'm going to help you," Dr. Mansfield said, his gaze low.

"Robbo? What the fuck is going on? Is he—?"

Robert nodded.

"Yeah, he is."

Cal frowned and nodded his head.

"Ah, good, because for a second there, I thought you were losing your fucking mind."

For good measure, Robert took a lateral step away from the doctor, who stayed in place. The movement sent pain shooting up his leg again. Leland Black may have cauterized the wound, but he hadn't done anything about the pain.

"Did he—?"

"No," Robert answered quickly, not wanting him to finish the sentence and have Dr. Mansfield say something that he wouldn't be able to explain later.

"What the fuck's wrong with your leg?" Shelly asked.

Robert resisted looking down at his jeans. Although covered, the lower part of his right leg looked more narrow to him nonetheless. That was another thing that he didn't have time, or perhaps even know how, to explain. He had a feeling deep down inside, spurred by his interaction with Leland, that he and Cal and Shelly would be best served purging the Seventh Ward of quiddity sooner rather than later.

There was something about the roiling sky of faces that made him think the longer the quiddity stayed here, the more powerful Leland would become.

"Nothing," Robert said quickly. "Just a story to *ha-ha* about another day. But right now, we have work to do."

He took a step forward, and was shocked to see that Shelly actually matched his movements…she took a step backward.

"I'm fine, Shelly. Really. We need to get to work."

Still, despite his words, he waited for her to make the first move. But she didn't; it was Cal who stepped forward and wrapped his arm around her shoulders.

"C'mon," he said to her loud enough for Robert to hear. "He's fine. Now let's go bust some ghosts."

She hesitated, but a slight tug spurred her to move. Robert didn't blame her for her apprehensive attitude. After all, he was limping, probably looked deathly pale from the blood loss, and there was the ghost of a dismembered doctor standing to his left.

Yeah, Robert probably would have been just a wee bit hesitant to do the tango with himself as well.

A loud grunt suddenly filled the hallway, and all of their eyes shot up, including Dr. Mansfield's, searching for its origins. It was louder than it had been before.

"We need to get out of the hallway," Robert said with a swallow after the sound faded. His eyes eventually landed on the rows of doors that lined both sides of the hallway. He wasn't keen on going back into a cell, but the prospect of being trapped out here by the sutured beast without a plan—like before—was unfathomable. "Let's get into one of those."

Cal raised an eyebrow.

"You have a key?"

Robert held up the keycard with Dr. Mansfield's photo on it.

Cal smirked.

"Sure as hell beats using a blowtorch."

Now it was Robert's turn to raise an eyebrow.

"Blowtorch?"

"It's a long story."

***

"Andrew Shaw wasn't even a real doctor," Dr. Mansfield said quietly. "He never finished his medical degree. But when he was first admitted here, I let him tag along. And for a while, everything was fine. To be honest, I think I was blinded by the fact that not only did I finally have some help in the ward from someone with at least some medical training, but, believe it or not, I liked him. You know, I wouldn't go as far to say that Hell Week for the SEALS is the same as medical school, but there are similarities. I mean, you are pushed hard…very hard, often by some dickhead doctor who just wants to cut his own workload and has no interest in actually training someone. Anyways, I guess I felt a little of what he felt, knowing how stressed and the sheer brunt of anxiety I faced way back when. I just felt sorry for him." Dr. Mansfield took a deep breath before continuing. "Maybe that's why I ignored the signs, or maybe he just hid them too well. God knows, he wouldn't have been the first. Some of my patients…well, let's just say that they can be very convincing. But inside, the personality that insists on being called Dr. Shaw, the one that we met here, had an obsession brewing. This too is not terribly uncommon for the recessive personality; they latch on to something—an idea, a notion, maybe—because they have little control over anything else. This usually doesn't pose much of an issue, except in the rare cases in which the recessive personality actually gains dominance. Which is what happened with Andrew—with Dr. Shaw."

The doctor paused as if remembering something specific, with Shelly, Cal, and Robert staring on.

"Dr. Shaw had this...this *notebook*, something that I..." He let his sentence trail off, then shook his head and composed himself. "He had this idea, see—this idea that split personalities weren't just mental, weren't just in his brain, but physical as well. As a child, he had undergone a lung transplant, and shortly thereafter he developed a split personality. *There's someone inside me*, he used to say over and over again. He blames the lung donor, but it wasn't that. The truth is, he was abused as a child, which is probably the trigger for his mental break— which, incidentally, was also the reason why he needed a lung transplant."

Dr. Mansfield sighed.

"But that's a story for another day...things were going fine, but then one day I lost my temper and pushed him too far. I should have remembered his case file, that the same sort of thing during his medical school that brought him here, to the Seventh Ward, got him kicked out of med school. Only, for whatever reason, when I pushed him in *this* place, Dr. Shaw came out. Maybe it was me, maybe it was the environment, or maybe it was just sheer bad luck. But for whatever reason, this time when Dr. Shaw came to the surface, he stayed."

The doctor stopped speaking again, and Robert thought that that was the end of the story, which was probably fitting because they were running out of time.

"Dr. Mansfield, do you—?"

Shelly held up her hand, stopping him. There was just enough light from the hallway coming in through the window for him to make out the stern expression on her pretty face.

"What happened next?" she whispered, voice hoarse.

Dr. Mansfield took a long time to answer, time that Robert thought was better served figuring out a plan of how to deal with the quiddity.

"He took pieces of me...he took pieces of my body and sutured them to others, trying to prove his insane theory."

"George," Shelly whispered.

Dr. Mansfield nodded.

"It didn't work...he was too aggressive, and I...I...I..."

He couldn't get the words out, and Robert wished that he could soothe the man. But he couldn't touch him—the last thing he wanted to do was go back to the horrible place with Leland Black and the flaming sky.

But then there was Amy. Leland had said she was okay, but...

Daddy, you promised...

"Please," Robert said at last, his own voice sounding strained. "No need to keep going."

Dr. Mansfield looked up at him, his eyes dark.

"But he didn't stop there...he seduced others—got them to come here with the help of Justine, who saw something in him, I guess. She used to be my nurse, but she was unstable, easily persuaded, gullible. And Dr. Shaw hacked—*Jesus*—he hacked the bodies up, stitching them together, naming his gruesome creations after me. They..." His body suddenly hitched, and Robert raised an eyebrow.

Dr. Mansfield was crying, and this realization gave Robert pause; he had no idea that ghosts could cry.

"That's who those other people are," Cal said softly.

Robert turned to him.

"What other people?"

Cal swallowed hard.

"In our cell...there were others, people with...with missing body parts, horribly disfigured people."

Dr. Mansfield nodded.

"Dr. Shaw's experiments."

The word made the back of Robert's leg twitch, but he resisted the urge to scratch.

An experiment...that's what I am now, too.

A guttural cry suddenly filled the hallway, and while it was muted by the heavy door to the cell, there was an urgency to it that hadn't been there before.

Robert swallowed hard, wondering what Dr. Shaw was doing to the man he called George...and what role the missing chunk of his calf was playing in it.

"We better hurry," he said quickly. "Cal, you and Shelly go find Justine. She's alive, that much I can confirm."

Cal looked uncertain, but Dr. Mansfield's nod seemed to convince him.

"Which is probably why Dr. Shaw is stuck here too—Justine keeps the narrative going. You guys deal with her. Dr. Mansfield and I will find Andrew Shaw and George and send them to the Marrow."

Something crossed over Dr. Mansfield's face when he said this, and Robert wondered, not for the first time, what the repercussions of bringing him back from the Marrow, from the clutches of the Goat, would be.

He made a mental note to ask Dr. Mansfield later, after this was all done.

"Robbo? Fuck, you sure? How—?"

Robert shook his head.

"I'm not sure, but—"

"We can just leave," Shelly said softly. "Can just go crawl back out the window the way we came in, get the *fuck* out of here."

It was Cal who answered.

"I won't—can't. Made a promise to those people—those *quiddity*—in the cell."

Robert nodded.

"And Dr. Mansfield saved me." He looked over at the man, whose pale cheeks were still moist from tears. "I won't leave him here any longer."

He stared at Shelly for a moment as she chewed on the inside of her cheek. Eventually, she nodded.

"Okay," she said softly. Then she slipped the bag off her shoulder and held it out to him.

For a moment, Robert thought this meant that she was going to flee and leave them here, and his heart sunk. But then she spoke again, and he took a deep breath.

Shelly wasn't going anywhere.

"You're gonna need this more than I do. Don't worry about Justine, we'll put that bitch in her place."

And then she reached out for him almost desperately, and Robert nearly lunged at her. He breathed her scent in deeply and then pulled back.

Staring into those green eyes, Robert was nearly overcome with a desire to kiss her. To press his lips to her bright red ones.

But the moment passed and they separated. Robert turned back to Dr. Mansfield.

"You said something about a notebook, Doc?"

The man nodded.

"Alright, let's grab that first...we're probably going to need it."

Chapter 34

CAL FOUND A FLASHLIGHT on a small table near the room that they had been confined in. It was a serendipitous finding, as he had sent the table spinning loudly when he had bumped into it in the dark. He also found his crowbar, which he promptly picked up and slid into the hidden pocket in the back of his pants. Only then did he ditch the black robe; not only were Shelly and Robbo right—it looked bloody ridiculous—but it was more restrictive than it appeared.

Even though they were now armed with one flashlight—having since given the other to Robert—they were hesitant to use it, for fear that Dr. Shaw or George might be near.

As it turned out, Justine wasn't too hard to find even in the dark. The problem was, neither was George.

"You hear that?" Cal asked quietly as they had made their way past the door that they had blown open and down a second hallway. This one was darker than the one that they had just come from, and narrower as well. There were also fewer rooms, irregularly spaced. They only needed to take a few steps before they knew where to focus their attention. Light splayed out through the rectangular window of the third of five doors.

Shelly nodded.

"I hear it," she whispered.

The sound of heavy, labored breathing, like someone having a hard time catching their breath after sprinting, infiltrated the otherwise silent hospital ward.

Crouching low to avoid being seen through the windows, they crept down the hallway with Cal taking the lead. He slipped the crowbar out from behind his back and gripped it with one hand, while Shelly followed closely, her hand against his back to remain in contact, and the other gripping the flashlight, ready to turn it on at a moment's notice.

As they neared the third door, the sounds of breathing got progressively louder.

Cal scurried beneath the window after indicating that Shelly should remain on the other side of the door. Then, with both of their backs pressed against the wall, he turned to face his friend.

The light coming from the window was weak, but being so close to it meant he was able to make out her face.

He had seen the exchange between Robert and Shelly when they had hugged, and it had hurt him deeply. He was the one that had brought Shelly in, and goddamn if he didn't long for that piece of ass. And besides, he was the one that spent nearly every day with her when Robert was locked upstairs in his room.

And yet when she looked at him now, she only looked scared. When she looked at Robert, however...

Shelly made a face, as if to say, *what the hell do we do now?*

Cal shrugged, and he regained his focus.

The breathing returned, and he was hard-pressed to believe that it was anyone *but* George, which was supposed to be Robert's problem. But Robbo had gone the other way with Dr. Mansfield—if Dr. Shaw and George were here, in the room just a foot or two away, there was only one thing that they could do: run. But just crouching there, backs against the wall, was serving them no good. And they had a flashlight, which might be used to blind them if they absolutely had to.

And the crowbar, they had that, too. Only the last time Cal had used it against George, it hadn't ended exactly the way he'd wanted. Maybe if they had the blowtorch...

Cal shook his head. They didn't have that anymore—Shelly had given her backpack to Robert.

He sighed deeply, then closed his eyes for a moment. When he opened them again, he pointed at the window, the universal sign for *I'll take a look*.

Shelly grimaced, clearly uncomfortable with the idea, and he watched as her two-handed grip on the flashlight tightened.

They had little other choice.

Steeling his nerves, Cal took three deep breaths, then slid up to a standing position, his thighs thanking him for the reprieve from squatting.

My body ain't made for shoveling. Or squatting. Or running, which I'm probably going to have to do in just a...

Before losing his nerve, he slowly turned his head and peeked into the room.

All of the blood immediately drained from his limbs, and it was all he could to hold on to the crowbar.

The scene inside the cell was incredibly bizarre...and horrific. Cal's eyes first went to the gurney, upon which the monster known as George lay. He was naked, his horrible stitched body, an amalgamation of others, on display. His eyes were closed, his head resting on one side. All of his other wounds, including the horrible, desiccated tear in his cheek, looked old, in some stage of rot or decay. Everything except for his right leg, that is. There was a hunk of flesh on his calf that looked fresher than the rest; it looked less gray, less *dead*. And there was blood-soaked gauze and towels underneath the foot.

I guess that's what all that howling was about.

He turned his attention to the other person in the room next, and relief washed over him when he realized that it was Justine.

Only that didn't last long—it was a transient, fleeting feeling. The nurse was sitting on a chair in the corner of the room, her back to him. She was in the process of getting dressed, of slipping her pale blue scrubs over her pale body. Cal retched as he caught sight of the state of her bare back.

Like George, her skin was a mess, a patchwork of stitches and scars that would have made a relief map of Utah look like a skating rink. Only this was different; George was a monster, a hideous freak that was long dead, while Justine...well, she was alive, wasn't she? Robert and Dr. Mansfield had seemed so certain of this.

There were pockmarks, deep groves in her back, some of which hadn't even healed over yet. Beneath the soft flesh of her right shoulder blade was a baseball-sized wound that was glistening that with every breath seemed to pucker ever so slightly.

Cal retched again, a visceral reaction that drew his gaze from the window. Blinking rapidly, he looked backed up again, avoiding eye contact with Shelly. In the process, however, the hand holding the crowbar dropped just a fraction of an inch, and it tapped against the door. It was the subtlest of sounds, a tiny 'ting' noise, that was barely audible. But the instant it happened, Justine's blonde head whipped around.

Cal should have dropped to the floor; if he had dropped, maybe Justine would have gone back to whatever horrible thing she'd been doing, passing the sound off as a rat or just the floor creaking.

Maybe she would have stayed in the room. But when Cal caught sight of the woman's chest, he froze again.

Justine's breasts were gone, replaced by horrible, taut flesh.

Clearly, she had been part of Dr. Shaw's experiments as well. And yet she had survived.

The woman's eyes bored into him, and this snapped Cal out of his revulsion stupor and he dropped.

But it was too late.

Justine had seen him, and she was coming to the door.

Chapter 35

"THAT'S IT, RIGHT THERE," Dr. Mansfield said, indicating the top drawer of a desk near the back of a small office. It was ironic that the office was smaller than even the cell he was trapped in previously—for all of the rumors about this place, it really did appear to be somewhere where the patients came first. The office was Dr. Mansfield's, but the placard with his name on it had been scrawled over in what Robert knew could only be blood and now read: SHAW.

"There?" Robert asked, feeling uneasy for some reason. He hadn't wanted to separate from his friends, but there was no way that he was going to send them to deal with George and Dr. Shaw. There was *no* way; after all, they were only here because of him.

Dr. Mansfield nodded, and Robert quickly walked over to it, careful to keep the flashlight beam low.

"Did you put it in here? Or did he?" he asked as he opened the drawer. It was full of random pieces of paper, which Robert shoved aside. He was looking for a blue notepad, the old-fashioned spiral kind.

"He did. After I saw the—well, after I found Dr. Shaw, he…he took me away. I never came back alive."

Robert paused, the strangeness of the words washing over him. If someone had said anything like this more than three months ago, he probably would have sent them here, the psychiatric ward—not to purge quiddity, but for them to be admitted. Now, however, they almost seemed normal.

Almost.

"Got it," he said, his hands closing on a worn blue folder, just as Dr. Mansfield had described. Robert pulled it out of the drawer. Curiosity overwhelmed him, and before they left the office in search of Shaw and his pet monster, he opened it.

He exhaled involuntarily as he flipped through the pages.

The top line of every page was a patient name, but the rest of the lines were all filled with the same sentence: *There's someone inside me…*

Robert quickly flipped through to the last page, but he realized that it was torn out.

"Missing page?" he asked, not really expecting to find anything of any insight, or even different from the scrawling that filled the rest of the book.

But Dr. Mansfield's face suddenly went dark, and Robert held the book up for the man to see.

"The last page?" the doctor asked softly.

Robert flipped the torn edge back and forth.

"Yeah, think so. Why?"

"Because, it—"

But another voice answered the question for him.

"—it was *his* page," Dr. Shaw said.

Robert dropped the book and whipped the flashlight up to eye level, while at the same time Dr. Mansfield spun around to face the voice.

Andrew Shaw was standing in the doorway of the office, hands at his sides, blood dripping from his fingers. As both men watched in horror, he slowly snaked his hand into the pocket of his lab coat.

Robert started to breathe quickly, unsure of what to do next.

What if he pulls out a weapon? A scalpel? Can he cut me? Can he cut Dr. Mansfield? Would it matter?

So many questions ripped through his mind that he locked up.

But thankfully Andrew didn't pull a weapon from his lab coat. Instead, he pulled a piece of paper.

"Andrew, you need to—"

Dr. Shaw stopped unraveling the paper and turned his gaze to Dr. Mansfield, his brow lowering.

"I told you to call me Dr. Shaw."

Then he went back to unfolding the piece of paper.

"This is craziness...think about what you're doing, Dr. Shaw. You were on a path to become a doctor—you were destined to help people, not harm them," Dr. Mansfield pleaded.

Andrew's expression went smug, and instead of answering, he read the paper instead.

"Patient #001, Dr. George Thomsen Mansfield. *There's someone inside me...*"

Robert slowly moved the flashlight away from Andrew's face as he continued to read that same sentence what seemed like dozens of times. He moved the beam of light back and forth around the man's chest with simple, subtle movements, changing the angle ever so slightly. Although the man wasn't completely solid, he wasn't as transparent as James or Patricia Harlop had been, either.

Something is changing, Robert thought suddenly. *And it has to do with the rift in the Marrow.*

These weren't the same quiddity...they were more real somehow.

More permanent.

Andrew finally finished reading, his expression proud as if he had just shared the most important medical discovery of the past century instead of just spouting gibberish.

"This...this isn't helping people. What you did to me wasn't helping. Neither was what you did to Justine, the others...you are supposed to help people," Dr. Mansfield continued. "Please, just hand me the paper."

Andrew turned to face the doctor, and for a brief second his expression went from smug to soft, sad even. It was clear to Robert in that moment that Dr. Mansfield was trying to appeal to Andrew, the other personality buried for all these years, and not to Dr. Shaw.

And to his untrained eyes, it appeared to be working.

When Dr. Shaw spoke next, his voice even seemed different.

"I just—I *wanted* to help people, Dr. Mansfield. To help people like me, people who were good, but who had someone else trapped in here." The man raised a finger and tapped at his temple, leaving a bloody smudge at his hairline.

"Yes, yes, that's right, Andrew. I know you wanted to help. That's why I took you under my wing, remember?"

Andrew nodded subtly.

"I asked you to help me because I knew you were good...and because you were smart, too."

Again, Andrew nodded.

"I just wanted to help..."

Dr. Mansfield stepped forward, intent on comforting the man who was on the verge of a breakdown, when Andrew slipped his left hand into the pocket of his lab coat. Just as Dr. Mansfield reached for him, Andrew leaned forward and put his right hand on the man's shoulder.

Although Dr. Mansfield was unaware of what was happening, Robert could see it all with vivid clarity.

"*No!*" he shouted, but it was too late.

Dr. Shaw's face broke into a lecherous grin as he slipped the scalpel from his pocket. Then he reared back and drove the glinting blade deep into Dr. Mansfield's guts, twisting and turning it as it slid into his body.

"I told you when I killed you the first time," Dr. Shaw hissed, "I *am* helping you."

Dr. Mansfield gasped and tried to pull away, but Andrew's grip on his shoulder and the scalpel held firm. Then the much stronger man, who Robert could have sworn appeared more solid than he had even just a few seconds ago, lifted his head skyward.

"George!" he yelled at the top of his lungs. A sinister grin formed on his lips as he turned back to Dr. Mansfield. "I'm going to enjoy killing you again, just like you're gonna *love* your visit with the Goat."

Chapter 36

CAL SWORE UNDER HIS breath, and then glanced at Shelly. She was staring at him, her thick red lips mouthing the words, *what the fuck?*

"She saw me," he whispered, "she fucking saw me."

Shelly started to stand, but Cal encouraged her to sit with several aggressive gestures.

"He's in there, too," he said, eyes wide.

There was no need to specify who 'he' was—the expression in his face made this abundantly clear.

"What the fuck do we do? Do we—?"

They heard a beep, and the door suddenly started to open. Both Cal and Shelly froze.

"Dr. Shaw?" Justine asked tentatively through the three-inch gap.

Cal, still crouched, tried to make himself as small as possible. Relief washed over him when he realized that even though their eyes had met, she didn't seem to have recognized him.

"Doctor? You—"

The door opened a little wider, and Justine stepped a foot into the hall. Cal tried to scoot away from her, but he was too slow and the toe of her worn sneaker bumped up against the crowbar.

"What's going on?"

Justine looked down, and this time when their eyes met, there was no question that she knew who he was. For such a large, damaged woman, she moved surprisingly quickly. It didn't help that Cal's legs were sore from squatting, either, and that he was leaning backward.

"George!" Justine screamed. "George, get the fuck out here!"

And then she pounced on Cal, and it was Cal's turn to call for help.

"Shelly!" he yelped a split second before she landed on him.

Cal wasn't one for exercise, health, and last but not least, fighting. So when he was confronted with a crazed two-hundred-pound psychopath bearing down on him, he did what anyone in his situation would have done. Instead of raising his arms, crowbar in hand, or trying to get out of the way, he attempted to catch her on his feet, and then fling her over his head.

He had seen it in a video game once, and it looked easy enough.

In real life, however, the result was a complete failure. Cal only got one leg up in time, and that wasn't nearly enough to support Justine. She collapsed on top of him, her weight forcing the air from Cal's lungs.

The nurse smelled foul, and as her hands came raining down on him, it was all he could do to turn his head to the side. Her nails raked deep into his cheek, immediately drawing blood. Cal tried to put his hands up to defend himself, but they were pinned beneath her chest and belly.

"Shelly!" he cried as Justine drove a hammer fist into the side of his face, speckling his vision with stars. In a desperate move, Cal lifted his hips and somehow managed to shift most of her weight toward the wall. Then he heard a click as the door to the operating room closed. At the same time, Shelly reared up, clasped both hands together, and raised them high over her head.

Cal closed his eyes in expectation of the massive blow.

A blow that never came.

Instead, he heard a dull 'thunk' and then felt all of Justine's weight pile down at once. And then the air was knocked out of him again.

Struggling to fill his lungs, Justine's awful breath accosted him as her cheek came to rest on his own. Cal opened his mouth to scream, but before the sound could exit, blood from Justine spilled onto his face, causing him to gag and cough.

What the—?

Cal opened his eyes, mere inches from Justine's, which were closed. Frantic, he bucked his hips, causing the nurse's unconscious body to rock just enough for him to scoot out from beneath her.

"Fuck, fuck, fuck!" he yelled, spitting blood onto the floor while at the same time wiping at his mouth with his hands.

He looked up and saw the impossible: Justine seemed to be levitating just a few inches from the ground, blood from the back of her head dripping off her sagging cheeks and forming a steady trail onto the floor. The skin around her eyes was turning blue, and her breathing was incredibly labored.

Cal again felt his stomach lurch.

How is this possible?

He raised his eyes a little higher and saw Shelly standing above Justine, her legs spread, the heavy flashlight in one hand, the end marred by red and flecks of pink. Her eyes were squinted, her expression fierce.

Cal gaped.

"You got beat up by a girl," Shelly said with a smirk. "A *fucking* girl."

Chapter 37

ROBERT'S FEET SEEMED TO be embedded in ice. He was still holding the flashlight in his hand, but it seemed wholly ineffective versus Andrew and his scalpel. His eyes darted about the room, looking for anything that he might be able to use, a welcome distraction to the confusion that washed over him.

Can Andrew kill Dr. Mansfield...again?

Both of the men were already dead, that much Robert was sure of. Everything else, however...

What he knew for certain was that he didn't want Dr. Mansfield to be sent to the Goat. The man deserved better than that. After all, he had saved Robert.

Now it was his turn to return the favor, if that was at all possible.

His eyes fell on the backpack that Shelly had handed him, and her voice ripped through his brain.

Blowtorch!

The ice that gripped his legs suddenly thawed and he scrambled for the blowtorch out of sheer instinct. He had no idea what he was going to do with it, but as Andrew drove the knife deeper and the blood began to flow out of Dr. Mansfield's mouth and drip to the floor, any semblance of rationality left him.

Robert somehow managed to light the blowtorch on the first try and it hissed to life, illuminating the room in a wash of yellow that battled with the incandescent blue from the flashlight that he had set down on the desk. The eerie lighting reminded him of the Marrow after Leland had showed up and the sky had changed from clouds to flames.

The light reflected off Dr. Shaw's eyes, making the dark orbs glitter as he continued to grind his hand back and forth.

His fist was almost completely buried inside Dr. Mansfield now.

Robert stepped from behind the desk, holding the blowtorch with the four-inch flame out in front of him.

"Andrew, let him go!" Robert shouted. Dr. Shaw's only response was to stare into Dr. Mansfield's eyes and drive the blade even deeper. A hollow croak joined the blood pouring out of Dr. Mansfield's mouth.

Robert took another step forward, and this time Dr. Shaw turned to face him.

The man was even more sinister now that his face was turned toward the flames; his entire pale face seemed to flicker and shimmer.

"You think that will hurt me?" he laughed a dry cackle. "Did you learn nothing, Robert Watts? Did Leland teach you *nothing*?"

Robert was advancing as the other man spoke, but at the mention of Leland's name and the resulting image of the man in the hat that flashed in his mind, he stopped.

Dr. Andrew Shaw laughed and twisted the knife again.

"You can't kill me with that," he said, lifting his chin toward the blowtorch. "*You* can't kill me at all."

Robert glanced at the flame and knew deep down that what the man was saying was right. The paltry comfort that it offered him was superficial; a torch would do nothing to a dead man like Shaw.

But the man's blade, on the other hand, seemed more than capable of harming Dr. Mansfield, who moaned and slumped.

Desperation overcame Robert as he stared into the psychopath's flickering face.

If the torch wouldn't help him, what would? How could he ever save his friends? His daughter?

He was on the verge of giving up, of resigning himself to using the blowtorch and seeing what happened, when Dr. Mansfield's mouth started to move.

There was no way for him to hear the man over the hissing of the torch, so he tried to read lips instead.

The boulder? The molder? The colder?

Robert squinted hard, knowing that at any moment Andrew could slip Dr. Mansfield off his blade and then come for him. And when he got to Robert, he wouldn't have to shiv him; all he would have to do was touch him and Robert would be back in Leland's grasp.

His eyes continued to whip around the room at a frenzied pace, until he got dizzy and he was forced to rest a hand on the desk to keep his balance.

I'm sorry, Cal. I'm sorry, Shelly. I'm —

But then his eyes fell on the blue notepad that he had taken from the desk earlier.

The folder!

Robert lunged for it.

Shelly's words from what seemed a lifetime ago sounded in his head.

You need to bind the quiddity to something...something that means something to them.

He grabbed the folder and held it up to Andrew like some sort of effigy. Dr. Shaw's expression, previously one of maniacal glee, suddenly became serious.

"Don't," he said simply. And then he used the hand that was holding Dr. Mansfield's shoulder to push him off the scalpel. Dr. Mansfield slumped to the floor, unmoving.

"Don't," the man warned.

Robert didn't hesitate. Before Andrew could leap at him, he brought the book up to the end of the blowtorch and set it alight.

"No!" Dr. Shaw bellowed. When the man was within a foot of Robert, he thrust the burning book at him and then scrambled backward.

Dr. Andrew Shaw couldn't help himself. He dropped the scalpel, then grabbed the flaming book with both hands, clutching it to his chest in an attempt to smother it.

Robert didn't know if quiddity were particularly flammable, or if it was just because Andrew Shaw had been bound to an object that meant something to him, but he ignited as if soaked in kerosene.

And judging by the way he cradled the burning book against his chest with both hands, it meant more than *something* to him.

It meant everything.

Dr. Shaw shuddered, and his figure all of a sudden became less *whole*. The man's eyes whipped up, and it was immediately apparent to Robert that the man with the flames leaping up his lab coat and licking at his face, melting his shaggy brown hair, wasn't Dr. Shaw anymore.

It was Andrew Shaw, the obedient, intelligent medical student that Dr. Mansfield had described.

Sadness unexpectedly overcame Robert as he watched the man's outline start to waver.

The man didn't say anything as he burned, which somehow made things worse. He didn't cry, he didn't scream, he didn't plead for his soul. He simply faded in silence, his body burning quickly, reminding Robert of the way the sky had looked in the Marrow, the way the tortured faces had grown and shrunk, bellowing in flames.

And then Andrew Shaw was gone; the only evidence that he had ever been there was a pile of soot in the center of the room.

Robert stared at that pile for a good minute, trying to understand what had just happened. Then he heard a soft moan, and remembered that Dr. Mansfield was still crumpled in a ball on the floor. He ran to him, crouching, nearly touching him before remembering.

"Dr. Mansfield?" he said, only partly expecting a response.

But Dr. Mansfield surprised him by raising his eyes and turning his head to face him.

"I'm sorry," the man said softly, which was followed by a cough and a thin stream of blood that trickled down his chin.

"Sorry? For what?"

"I—I—" But the man couldn't finish.

"It's okay, Dr. Mansfield," Robert consoled him. He gave the doctor's body a onceover, trying to figure out what the fuck he was going to do. The man was on his side, his knees curled up to his chest, his hands clutching his midsection. Blood was starting to pool beneath his body.

"What's going to happen next?" Dr. Mansfield asked unexpectedly.

Robert hesitated, and then answered with the first thing that came to mind.

"I don't know…"

But Robert thought that he knew. Inside, he *knew*.

This man wasn't going to the serene shores of the Marrow.

No, Dr. George Mansfield was going to the other place. The one with the flames, the faces in the fire, the muddy hands on the shore. He was going to see Leland Black.

Bringing Robert back meant that he was destined to answer to the Goat.

"Doctor, I—*Doctor!*"

The man's eyes rolled back into his head and went a pitch black, whites and all.

"Doctor!"

Robert felt a tingling in his lids, and knew that tears were coming. But then a deep, thundering cry filled the Seventh Ward and he forced them away.

There was more work to do.

There was another George that needed to be purged.

Chapter 38

"**WHAT DO WE DO?** What the fuck do we do?" Cal begged desperately. A shout for George rang out in the hallway, and he quickly glanced back into the room. The monster was still tied down, but he was awake now and pulling hard against the restraints. Judging by the way the leather was beginning to split, it was clear that they wouldn't hold for long.

"Shit, Shelly. What the *fuck* do we do?"

His eyes darted from Shelly, who was still standing in that same dominant pose, the flashlight gripped in one hand, to Justine.

The woman wasn't levitating as he had first thought, but she *was* choking to death. Her face had turned a deep blue, and bubbles had started to form in the corners of her lips.

Her scrubs had gotten trapped in the door when it closed, and now it was holding her parallel to the ground, the V-neck opening pressing into her throat, cutting off her air supply.

"Let the bitch die," Shelly said bluntly.

Cal made a face and his eyes whipped about again.

What the hell should we do?

Justine was probably the worst of the bunch, worse than even George because she was *alive*, but it still didn't feel right to just let her die here like this.

He reached up and pulled at his hair.

"Fuck," he shouted.

There was the sound of stirring in the room, but he didn't dare look. Whatever they were going to do, be it leave or free Justine, they had to do it quickly.

Cal brought a hand from his head to the wound on his face, hissing at the pain. There was no doubt that Justine's handiwork would leave a mark.

Not as bad as George, but bad nonetheless. Cal was suddenly reminded of Danny Dekeyser, the man who had provided the face that was stitched to the monster inside the cell.

You promise you will help us? That you will send us home?

Cal's eyes whipped down to Justine as a thought occurred to him. It was a long shot, but if it worked, it would solve a lot of their problems.

"Quick," he said, dropping to one knee in front of the dying nurse. "Help me get her out of the door."

At first, Shelly didn't move and Cal glanced up at her.

"Please, Shel, I have a plan."

Again, nothing.

"For fuck's sake, Shelly, just give me a fucking hand!"

Shelly finally moved to action, quickly reaching for the door. She tried to pull it open, but it wouldn't budge.

"Get the keycard," Cal said, lifting Justine's head. A horrible wheeze escaped her as she finally drew in a full breath. Her blue pallor faded slightly, and for a second Cal thought that she was going to wake and attack him again. But as her breathing regulated, she remained unconscious.

Shelly dropped to the floor and began searching through the woman's pockets. Justine's head was so heavy that Cal had to use both hands to hold it up.

"You find it?"

"Looking...fuck."

"What?"

Shelly flicked a taut wire that ran from the waist of Shelly's scrubs to the door. Like the scrubs themselves, the keycard was stuck inside the room. Which meant that they were going to have to cut the woman's clothes off her.

There was a loud snapping sound from inside the room followed by a deep, resonating groan.

And it also meant that George would be able to use the card to get out.

"Cut the clothes off, Shelly, hurry!"

She looked at him, an eyebrow raised.

"With what? You think I've got knitting shears in my back pocket?"

Cal swore under his breath and looked around.

"Shine the flashlight over there," he instructed, indicating behind him.

Shelly obliged, and the light reflected off the crowbar.

"There! Grab the crowbar. Use the sharp end to tear the fabric."

Shelly ran to it and brought it back.

Cal, still holding the nurse's head so that she could breathe, indicated a spot by the neck where the fabric had frayed slightly.

"Start there. Once you make a hole, we can just rip it."

There was another snap from inside the room—which made two. Cal only hoped that it was George's legs straps, because if they were his arms, then he would be able to unbuckle the legs.

And then they would have seconds and not minutes.

Shelly, sensing his urgency, put the flashlight on the ground and used both hands to plant the curved end of the crowbar in the frayed area. She pushed hard, and Justine groaned.

"What?" she asked when Cal gave her a look.

Then she pulled, and Cal heard the satisfying sound of fabric tearing. He let her head go again, and together he and Shelly tore the shirt from her body. When they were done, Justine fell face first onto the hard linoleum, and Cal heard a crunch of what he suspected was her nose breaking.

Meh, she deserved that.

"Okay, quick, grab a leg."

But again, Shelly hesitated. In fact, she appeared frozen.

Cal reached for the flashlight and shone it up at her. Not even the bright light directly in her eyes elicited a response.

Her expression was one of pure horror. At first, Cal thought that she was staring at the door, that George was coming out, but then he realized that she was looking at Justine's back.

Cal couldn't stomach another glance, as just the recollection of the gaping wounds, the scars, the stitches, was enough to force him to swallow hard.

"Don't look," he said between gulps. "Don't look, just *pull*."

Shelly blinked, and held an arm up in front of her face to shield herself from the bright light and to block out the gruesome sight.

With her other hand, she reached down and grabbed one of Shelly's legs while Cal took the other.

Both of them stood and started to pull, grunting as they dragged Justine across the floor. A quick glance back revealed a meandering trail of blood from her face on the dark tiles.

"Where are we going?" Shelly grunted.

Cal gave a stiff yank, and they picked up the pace, now at least a dozen feet from the door to the cell.

"Back to—"

But then they heard a beep, and Cal's forehead broke out in a cold sweat.

"Pull!" he yelled. "Shelly, fucking *pull!*"

Cal and Shelly had just yanked Justine's unconscious body through the threshold of their cell before George rushed by.

Heaving, sweating, Cal pushed his back against the wall, praying that the monster didn't see him. For at least a minute, he stood there with Shelly beside him, waiting and listening. Even after the monster's footsteps had receded out of earshot, they remained rooted in place.

Chapter 39

ROBERT FROZE.

Even as the heavy, off-balance footsteps neared, he couldn't find it in himself to actually move. He knew that he should run, or at worst hide behind the desk before George approached, but he didn't.

Fear was part of it, but there was something else, too, something that he didn't quite understand.

George turned the corner and filled the doorway of the office, his heavy breathing audible even over the hissing of the blowtorch that sat unattended on the desk.

They locked eyes, and Robert did his best to hold his ground. It was an unnerving experience, something that took all of his effort, particularly given the horrible stitches and the sloped, uneven shape of his head.

"I'm going to tear your heart out," George said at last. The beast took an off-balance step forward, but still Robert didn't move. His lack of apparent fear seemed to render George uncertain, as he stopped after just one step. It was then that Robert saw the bloody calf muscle on George's right leg.

His calf muscle.

Robert swallowed hard and then instinctively pulled up his right pant leg. He wasn't sure why he did this—perhaps he thought that it might incite some strange sort of kinship, seeing as George now possessed a part of him, or maybe it was just to make it known that they had both been injured by the same person. But when George's dark black eyes fell on the wound, they suddenly went wide.

George gasped, and he shuffled backward awkwardly.

"You've been touched by him! By the Goat!"

Robert's eyes quickly flicked down, and locked on the three gray, elongated claw marks.

"I won't go back," George bellowed, before turning and running in his off-balance gait out of the room.

Robert waited for a moment, contemplating the monster's words.

Back? He's been before? I thought no one came back...

But Robert himself was clear evidence that one could come back.

Something came over him then, a sudden desire—need, even—to send George back to the Marrow. To banish him.

And that time was of the essence.

There was no way that he could let this quiddity remain with the living.

Robert grimaced at the pain in his leg, then hurried after the lumbering monster, his hand closing on Dr. Mansfield's keycard that was still tucked away in his pocket.

***

Under normal circumstances, Robert would have had no problem catching the shambling beast, especially given the man's uneven legs. But his own leg started to ache the farther he went up the embankment behind the hospital. And the cold wind biting into his skin in the dark only seemed to accentuate the feeling.

It was almost as if he could feel Leland's fingers still gripping his flesh, searing it with his poisonous grasp.

George had stumbled out of sight some time ago, but it wasn't difficult to follow his path; he was large and ungainly, and even if he didn't make obvious tracks through the over-grown vegetation, the sound of him crashing through would have led Robert to him.

The moon shone brightly overhead as Robert crested the top of the hill at the back of Pinedale Hospital, huffing and breath-ing heavily, rubbing the sore back of his leg where a chunk of his calf was missing. Thankfully it was late fall, and the moon-light shattered through the leafless trees like misty splinters.

Robert's pace was slow now, the back of his leg seizing every few steps. It took nearly a half hour before he saw it, and if it weren't for the broken trees and thick footprints, he probably would have walked right by.

Buried in the side of a small hill, barely visible amidst an outcropping of rocks and thick vegetation, was the door to a small, dilapidated shack.

Robert recalled what Dr. Mansfield had said to him, about being dragged from the hospital and then tortured in a shack in the woods.

This was *that* shack, he knew.

And George was inside.

Robert shuffled as quietly as his aching body would allow to the side of the cabin. Then he chanced a look in the window. The glass was scratched and filthy, and he had only a small clear area by which to make out the interior.

There was blood everywhere; brown smudges on the walls, on the floor, on the side of the ceramic basin. As if that weren't enough, there was a large pile of rags in the corner that were completely soaked with the stuff. Robert also caught sight of a small table—a modified picnic table—with what looked like a pile of extension cords sitting atop it.

And tools: there were various surgical tools strewn haphazardly about the place, filling nearly every square inch of dusty counter space.

Robert's breath caught in his throat when his eyes finally fell on George, who was curled into a mountain of a ball in the corner.

He appeared to be weeping.

Robert swallowed and then stepped into the cabin.

Chapter 40

IT WAS JUSTINE THAT snapped Cal and Shelly out of their paralysis.

The woman groaned, and tried to lift her head off the floor. Her first attempt failed; her hair was gummy with blood and it clung to the floor before pulling her back down again. She was successful on her second attempt.

Shelly elbowed him in the side, indicating that now was the time to enact his master plan. He could tell by the grimace on her face that she wasn't hopeful. As if to reinforce this point, she grabbed the flashlight from his hand and gripped it tightly, poised to brain Justine again.

"Point it at her," Cal ordered.

The light was so bright that Justine hissed and turned her face away from them.

"Get up," Cal ordered. "Get the fuck up."

Justine spat a thick glob of blood onto the floor and then groaned as she made it to her knees. Cal could barely look at her with the holes in her back that wheezed and hissed with every breath.

How is she still alive?

With a labored grunt, Justine pulled herself to her feet, only then turning to face them. Justine wasn't shy; on the contrary, she knew that she looked hideous, her scarred body a mess, and she held her arms wide to show them her nude form in all its bruised and battered glory. A leer started to form on her face, revealing cracked front teeth that were stained a deep crimson.

"George is gonna get you," she said. Her voice was nasal, her nose bent a quarter inch to the left. "He's gonna get you, and then he's gonna fuck you up."

Shelly raised the flashlight and aimed it directly into her eyes. Justine hissed again, and brought her forearm up to cover her face. While she was distracted, Shelly looked over at Cal.

Cal nodded, as if to say, *I got this.*

Somewhere on the other side of the ward, George cried out, and Cal smiled.

"Looks like your friend Frankenstein is occupied."

Justine laughed.

"He's gonna get you. After he's done with your friend Robert, he's gonna get you."

Cal cleared his throat.

"Danny, you still here?"

The smile suddenly fell off Justine's face.

"Danny?"

Shelly shot him a look, but he ignored her.

Cal thought he knew what Danny and the other quiddity wanted most, what meant something to them.

And they all had it in common.

There was a flicker of movement behind Justine as Danny stepped forward, his mangled face bathed in shadows.

"I'm here," he said softly.

"Good. And what about your friends? They here too?"

Justine lowered her arm and glanced around nervously. For a second, Cal thought she might run, and he prepared himself to step in her way if she bolted toward the door.

As an answer, more of Justine and Dr. Shaw's victims stepped out of the shadows.

"No," Justine moaned softly. "No."

"Oh, yes," Cal replied with a smile.

And then he felt Shelly's hand on his shoulder. He looked at her, and she was smiling now too.

She understood.

The one thing that these quiddity wanted most of all was the life that was stolen from them prematurely. And while Cal couldn't provide them that, he could give them someone living. Someone that meant something to them, that they could bind to, something that they could ride all the way to the Marrow.

And then, as Cal had feared, Justine tried to run, but Danny was too quick. He reached out and his hand dug into Justine's shoulder. The woman screamed and tried to squirm away, but George's brother leapt from the shadows and wrapped a heavily muscled arm around her waist. Her nails scraped at the limb, but unlike the marks that they had made on Cal's face, they did little damage to the heavily muscled arm.

More arms and limbs appeared from the darkness, and soon all of the trapped souls of the Seventh Ward that Justine and Dr. Shaw had tortured for nearly a decade came forward.

And they all wanted a piece of her.

They dragged her to the ground, their hands gripping and pulling, punching and grabbing. She continued to scream, but Cal blocked out the sound.

Something yanked Justine toward the dark recesses of the cell, and Shelly lowered the flashlight a few inches. Before she was pulled completely away, however, Danny turned to him and stared into his eyes.

The man's whites were gone, replaced by simple black orbs.

Thank you, he mouthed.

And then they receded into the darkness.

"Come on," Cal said, turning to Shelly. He grabbed her arm and gently spun her toward the doorway. "Let's go find Robbo."

Arm in arm, they left the room to the sound of tearing flesh and a woman's screams.

You got what you deserved, bitch.

Chapter 41

"IS HE REALLY GONE?"

Robert nodded.

"Sent him back— he won't hurt you anymore."

The beast towering over him seemed to smile...if such a facial expression was possible on his mangled features. George's eyes were solid black orbs in his head. Even the one on the left side, the one that had a sutured flap of skin that wasn't his own, was solid, unblinking.

"He made me do those things...he has a way..." His sentence trailed off.

Robert swallowed hard.

"You have to go now," he said, trying to sound calm and assertive at the same time.

George's answer was immediate and unrelenting.

"No."

Robert had thought it might come to this. He racked his brain for ideas, a notion of how to send this man on his way to the Marrow. His eyes darted about the room, but nothing seemed to have any personal value at all...just surgical tools and bloody rags. There wasn't even a toilet, just a rusted, foul-smelling basin in the corner.

"You *have* to go, George."

Something flickered over the man's face, and Robert knew in that instant that the man was thinking about Leland Black; the man in the hat and the faded jean jacket, the one with a face so horrible that it seemed to have all but erased itself from Robert's memory.

Slowly, the beast shook his head.

"They call me George, but that's not my name." He raised his left arm, the thin, black one, then flicked at the hole in the side of his face. "I don't know who I am anymore. Dr. Shaw...he...I've had it just doing as I'm told. I won't go."

"You have to—"

"No," George repeated, a little louder this time. He began to stand taller, too, stretching to his full height. A culmination of others or not, he was an impressive, if repulsive, sight.

Robert tried to stand firm, not to flinch, but his heart had started to race in his chest. And his calf—by God, his calf *ached*.

What can I use? What can I use?

George stretched his lower jaw, causing the last of the stitches holding that side of his face together to tear. He was left with a gash that ran nearly to his temple, giving him an even more horrific smile.

"If I go," he threatened in his airy voice, his hands balling and starting to make fists, "I'm taking you with me."

Robert felt his heart skip a beat.

There was no way Robert was going back to the Marrow...not now, at least. One day for Amy, but not today.

A sudden, stabbing pain in his ankle brought him to one knee. He cried out, his hand immediately going to the spot.

George didn't seem interested.

"You have two choices, Robert Watts: one, you leave me here now and never return to the Seventh Ward or Pinedale Woods; or, two, I grab your puny shoulders and take you with me on a journey from which you will never return." His eyes did the impossible and seemed to darken even more. Then George took another step forward, closing the distance between them to less than four feet. The stench emanating from him was truly foul. "And trust me, it's not a place you want to go."

Grimacing, Robert raised his gaze and his eyes fell on the blood trickling down the back of George's leg—from his calf.

Robert's calf.

And in that moment, he knew what meant something to George; or, more specifically, what meant something to *him*. After all, George had a part of Robert sutured to him—he was part Robert.

So what meant something to Robert was important to George, too.

"What's your decision, Robert?"

Robert slowly forced himself to his feet again. Then he slowly snaked a hand into the front pocket of his jeans and pinched the picture therein between two fingers.

"Robert?" George shouted again.

Robert pulled the photograph out of his pocket and brought it up to eye level. The sight of his daughter's heart-shaped face drew a tear to his eye. He sniffed and wiped it away with the back of his hand.

"That's it, then? You're going to give up this world?" George said, misinterpreting his gesture.

Robert took a deep breath.

"I have—" His chest hitched. "—I *had* a daughter," he corrected himself. He turned the square photograph around and showed it to George.

It was impossible to tell if the man smirked or not given his mangled face, but Robert thought he might have.

"I don't give a shit about your daughter."

"Please, just take a look."

George growled, but for some reason, he reached forward and snatched the photo from his hand.

And now it was Robert's turn to smile.

"I don't—" George started to say as he flung his massive hand to one side, intent on throwing the photo away. But it seemed to be stuck to his fingers. "What the fuck?"

He whipped his hand again, but it still wouldn't come off. The man's black eyes shot up.

"What did you do to me?"

It was only then that George lowered his gaze to stare at the photograph that seemed fused to his fingers.

"Amy?" he whispered. The words sounded foreign to him, and the fact that this *thing* knew his daughter's name caused Robert's brow to furrow.

As he watched on, George started to shudder, his form, his *quiddity*, becoming more and more transparent. The man threw his head back and howled so loudly that it made Robert's molars tremble.

His eyes darted to the photograph that had seemingly glued itself to the man's hand.

This was the second time that Amy had saved him, and for that he was forever grateful.

He was brought back to Amy's voice he had heard in the Marrow, begging him, telling him that he had promised that she would be safe. And that was only moments before the man in the hat had appeared, sitting atop Patricia's tombstone.

Anger suddenly flooded over Robert, and he leaned in close, staring into George's coal-black eyes.

"Give a message to the Goat for me when you see him. Tell him—tell him that this is *my* picture," he hissed, jabbing a finger at the photograph in George's fading hand, "and this time I'm coming for *him*."

Chapter 42

"HOW'S THAT FOR A Sunday afternoon?" Cal asked as he pulled the door open to the Harlop Estate.

Exhausted, he veritably stumbled over the threshold, with Robert and Shelly in tow.

"Wait...it's Sunday?" Shelly asked as she collapsed onto the couch.

"No fucking clue."

Cal went straight to the liquor cabinet, but stopped halfway there and clutched his chest. Robert watched him closely, thinking that maybe he was having a heart attack.

"Cal?"

He was way too young for one, but given what they had seen...

Thankfully, Cal shook his head and started walking again, muttering something about being out of shape. As he poured two glasses of Glenlivet, the good stuff, the 30-year-old bottle, he addressed Robert.

"Man, it's about time I got back into shape...you interested, Robert? You know, pump some iron?"

Robert limped his way to the loveseat and flopped down on it. It felt so good to be sitting somewhere comfortable, even if it was a dusty, sixty-year-old suede loveseat.

"*Back* into shape?"

"Yeah, that's right, *back*. Don't you remember me in high school?" He walked over and handed the drink to Robert, who took it and sipped. Cal's eyes flicked to Shelly.

"Oh, yeah, you were jacked."

"Whatever," Cal said, finding his own seat. "Just for that comment, we are going to start with leg day."

Robert sighed and instinctively rubbed his calf.

"Very funny," he grumbled.

"What about me? No drink for me?" Shelly asked, reminding them that she was also present.

Cal didn't immediately answer, so Shelly reached out and promptly took the glass from him.

"Hey!"

She ignored him and smelled the liquid dramatically before taking a sip.

"I prefer beer, but this shit ain't bad."

Cal laughed and started to stand, intent on getting himself a new drink.

"Robbo, one thing I learned from this whole thing is that you do *not* want to fuck with this girl. Man, she was lethal with that flashlight. I mean, she wanted to..." As his words bordered on the serious, on reflecting the horrors that they had all experienced, he let his sentence trail off.

They needed some time off, time in which their thoughts weren't imbued with dead people.

Cal poured his scotch in silence, and they sat on their respective seats silently drinking for some time. Exhaustion engulfed them like a thick fog.

It was Cal who finally broke the silence.

"That was fucked up," he said simply.

Robert felt himself nodding.

"Is that it, then? Are we done with all this ghost shit?" he continued.

No one answered.

Robert wanted to say, *yeah, we're done,* but his thoughts kept turning back to Amy's voice coming from the fiery sky above.

No, I'm not done with this just yet.

"Maybe," Shelly answered, finishing her scotch. "I'm going to bed," she said, then pointed at Cal. "You better put something on those cuts on your face or it'll scar, and then I'll start calling your ass George."

With that, she left the room, leaving Cal to finger the scratch marks that Justine had raked across his cheek.

"Hilarious," Cal grumbled.

"I'm—" Robert started, but a knock at the front door interrupted him. He stood quickly, too quickly, and he immediately fell back down again, pain flaring up his leg. "I'll get it," he said between clenched teeth.

Cal eyed him suspiciously, but let him to go to the door by himself. It was, after all, technically his house.

It would have been a lie if Robert said that he was surprised to see Sean Sommers standing on the porch, wearing the same stupid suit and jacket and navy peacoat. His firm, thin-lipped expression was also predictable.

"Robert," the man said simply, holding out an envelope. Robert took it and looked inside. There was a check for 100k, as promised, written on a check for a bank he didn't immediately recognize.

Damn, you're quick.

"Thank you," Sean said with a curt nod, and then turned to leave.

Robert reached out for him, but the man pulled away.

"Not so fast." Robert glanced back into the estate, and even though Shelly was upstairs and Cal was still in the front room, he was concerned about sensitive ears. He stepped onto the broken cement steps and closed the door behind him. "You promised to answer some of my questions."

Sean turned back and inspected Robert.

"*A* question," he corrected him. "I promised that I would answer *a* question."

Robert nodded and swallowed. He had had a lot of time to think of his query on their long ride back to Hainsey County, and he had eventually come up with something.

"The man in the hat and the jean jacket," he began, lowering his voice several octaves, "Leland Black...who is he? Is he the devil of some sort? Are you God?"

Sean's eyes narrowed and he remained silent for so long that Robert thought that maybe his question was too broad, offensive, maybe, and that the man wasn't going to answer him.

But eventually, Sean did speak, and Robert listened.

"God? Me?" he chuckled. "No, Robert, I am not God. There *is* no God. At least, if there is, I've never met him. And what is the Devil without God?"

Robert narrowed his eyes. He didn't care for the ambiguous answer.

"Well then, what is he? What the *hell* is the Goat?"

Sean's expression remained flat and there was another uncomfortable pause.

"You promised—"

"Leland Black is your father, Robert."

Robert recoiled.

"He's *what?*"

His thoughts immediately turned to his father, or the image of the man that had died when he was only ten. A short, balding man with an infectious, rumbling laugh and eyes that glittered even at night.

"He's not—he's not my *father*," he said quickly.

Sean shrugged.

"Think, Robert. If you think about it long enough, you might remember."

Robert just stared, his head suddenly feeling light from fatigue, pain, and confusion.

Sean took this as his cue to leave, and started to turn. Robert wanted to stop him, but his mind was soupy.

Think about it? My dad was not the man in the Marrow. My dad was a good man.

Sean was halfway down the driveway before Robert snapped out of it.

He was no longer concerned with anyone in the estate hearing him.

"Wait!" he shouted. "Sean, *wait!*"

The man didn't turn.

"You can't just drop that bomb and leave. What do you mean he's my father? *Sean!*"

When the man still didn't turn, Robert started descending the steps, grimacing at the pain in his calf.

With every step, his vision became increasingly red.

"Well, what about Danny Dekeyser, then? He was a good man...you—what—fucking sent him there to do what? To clean the place, even though you knew what was hiding in the Seventh Ward?"

Sean finally stopped, and Robert was encouraged to continue.

"Yeah, Cal and Shelly saw him. Spoke to him. Described a fucking guy just like you who paid him to clean the place. So that's what you're into now, sacrifices? Is that what you're all about?"

In the back of his mind, Leland Black's words started to echo.

How much do you really *know about Sean Sommers, Robert?*

This time, Sean turned, the expression on the man's face catching Robert by surprise; it was soft, almost caring.

Then it hardened.

"Danny was dying—he had terminal cancer. I gave him an opportunity, a decision to leave his wife and daughter with some cash when he goes." Sean shrugged. "Like you, I gave him a choice. He knew the risks."

For some reason, this comment made Robert even angrier.

"Risks? *Risks?* Do you even know what we faced in the Seventh Ward? Huh?"

Sean simply stared, and Robert threw his hands up.

"You know what? I don't need you. I don't need you to go *back.*"

The man's face darkened and he shook his head.

"You'd be best served not to go back, Robert. Not to see *him.* There is a rift in the Marrow—there's something brewing. And every time you go, you make the link between this world and *his* world stronger. Do us all a favor and don't go back—*ever.*" The man paused for a moment before continuing, allowing his words to sink in. "If you think your father Leland is the devil, take a moment to consider what that makes you, Robert."

With that, the man spun and continued toward the iron gates at the front of the Harlop Estate.

"You can't walk away from this! Sean! *Sean!* You can't run away from this—not while he has Amy!"

This time, however, the man kept walking, leaving Robert alone to stare at the exhaust from the black Buick as it sped away.

Epilogue

LELAND BLACK STOOD ON the shores of the Marrow, staring out over the calm waves. He took a deep breath and shut his eyes. There was a girl sitting on his lap, and he reached out and stroked her blonde hair.

"It's okay, don't be afraid," he whispered.

When he opened his eyes again, serenity had vanished. In its place, the sky had become an inferno.

Lightning ripped through the air, which was promptly followed by a soft thump from somewhere behind him. Leland gently eased the girl to her feet and then he himself stood.

Even before he turned, he knew who was standing behind him.

Dr. Shaw's eyes were downcast, his complexion clammy. He opened his mouth to say something, but the Goat raised a hand and the man's mouth snapped shut.

Another bolt of lightning struck, and George appeared beside Dr. Shaw.

Leland observed both of them for a moment, taking in their revolting appearances with a scowl etched on his face hidden beneath the shadow of his black, wide-brimmed hat.

He walked up to Dr. Shaw and ran a pointed talon across the man's cheek, sending a shiver up his spine.

"You failed, Andrew," Leland said softly.

"They were—they were...I didn't—"

Leland moved behind Dr. Shaw and cut his words off by drawing a line across the man's throat, slicing it from ear-to-ear.

Andrew gasped, and tried to hold his neck, to force the gushing blood back in. With a growl, Leland opened his palm and raised it upward. Andrew levitated for a moment before ascending into the flames, his face incorporating with all of the other tortured souls that ebbed and flowed in the fire.

"I've had enough of you."

Leland turned his attention to George next. For all of the man's size and terror-inducing appearance, he was visibly shaking in front of the man in the hat and faded jean jacket.

"And you," the Goat whispered. "You were duped, weren't you? But loyal to the end, no?"

George bowed his head in shame.

Leland toyed with the beast, reaching out with a finger. George visibly recoiled from the digit, clearly thinking that his throat would be slit next, but instead Leland sliced the remaining sutures above his ear.

A hunk of rotting flesh fell away, landing in the tar beneath his feet. Frenzied hands snatched it up, pulling it down into their depths.

"He said—he said that he was coming for you," George said. With a trembling hand, he held out a small square photograph, which Leland snatched.

It was a passport photo of Amy.

Leland stared at that photo for a long time.

"Go join the others," he whispered, eyes still locked on Amy's face. "I have plans for you yet. You and Andrew and James Harlop. This isn't over."

He raised his hand again as he had done with Andrew, and George started to lift off the ground. But before sending him to the fire above, he spotted something on his calf.

He made a 'stay' gesture, then reached out and tore off the newly sutured hunk of meat. George cried out, but Leland didn't even look at him as he raised his hand again and George ascended into the flames.

As Leland observed the piece of flesh in his taloned hand, a smile crept onto his face.

"You won't need to come to me—I have a piece of you now. And I can find you." He put the photograph in his pocket. "*Tsk, tsk.* You can't hide from the Goat, Robert Watts."

Leland offered a dry chuckle and walked back to the girl, who was obediently standing where he had left her. When he neared her, Leland pushed the brim of his hat up to reveal his horrific face.

The girl didn't flinch.

"You can't hide from Leland Black, Robert."

He brought the girl into his embrace, and stroked her head again as he stared out over the soothing waves.

"Isn't that right, Amy?"

Her answer was immediate.

"Yes, Grandpa."

End

Author's Note

The idea for THE SEVENTH WARD came to me during research for a completely unrelated topic. I came across the idea that organs can have a memory of sorts, dubbed 'cellular memory theory', which *may* influence recipient behavior and or personality. Yeah, I stretched this idea to the extremes when I conjured up Andrew Shaw, but that's what fiction's for, isn't it?

The Haunted Series is far from over. As I write these tales about Robert, Shelly and Cal—which, to be honest are quickly becoming favorites of mine—I realize that there is much more to be written in their world. Consider it a calling from the Marrow, if you will, but I see more than the four books I have promised in this Series. Right now, you can pre-order the third book, SEAFORTH PRISON, on Amazon. It's due out in December.

And to all my fans of the *Insatiable Series* and *The Family Values Trilogy*, I haven't forgotten about you; STITCHES and DAUGHTER will be out soon, I promise.

As always, reviews are very much appreciated. And if you want to pop in and say hi, head on over to my Facebook page (@authorpatricklogan) or drop me a line at patrick@ptlbooks.com. I reply to everyone, even mean people (but don't be mean).

You keep reading, and I'll keep writing.

Best,
Patrick
Montreal, 2016

CPSIA information can be obtained
at www.ICGtesting.com
Printed in the USA
LVOW12s1833060717
540469LV00005B/896/P